BUT NOT
FOR ME

BUT NOT
FOR ME

•

Mona Ingram

AVALON BOOKS
NEW YORK

Published by Thomas Bouregy & Co., Inc.
160 Madison Avenue, New York, NY 10016

Library of Congress Cataloging-in-Publication Data

Ingram, Mona.
    But not for me / Mona Ingram.
        p.   cm.
    ISBN 978-0-8034-9885-3 (acid-free)
    1. Women cooks—Fiction.   2. British Columbia—Fiction.
I. Title.
    PR9199.4.I54B88 2008
    813'.6—dc22   2007037209

PRINTED IN THE UNITED STATES OF AMERICA
ON ACID-FREE PAPER
BY HADDON CRAFTSMEN, BLOOMSBURG, PENNSYLVANIA

For my sis,
who always took care of me

Prologue

"You're not really leaving, are you?"

Erin glanced up to see Crystal standing in the doorway, lower lip trembling convincingly. How many times over the past ten years had that ploy worked? And how many times had she glimpsed a spark of triumph after she gave in to her sister's wishes? Well not today. She checked one last time that she'd packed everything, her stomach fluttering with excitement at the thought of what she was about to do.

"Oh, I get it!" Crystal struck a defiant pose, one hand on her hip. "You're doing this to frighten me. That's what it is."

Smiling to herself at her sisters' theatrics, Erin walked to the foyer, setting her large duffel bag by the front door. This was the part that hurt but she knew deep down that she had to get away. Both for her own sake as well as her sister's.

"Aren't you going to say anything?" Crystal trailed behind, her petulant voice grating in Erin's ears.

She turned to her sister. "We've been over this so many times, Crys. What more do you want me to say?"

"I want you to say you're not leaving. I want you to stay here and take care of me."

Erin took a deep, steadying breath. "Has it ever occurred to you that I've been taking care of you for the past nine years? You were only eleven when Mom died. You needed me then, but you don't need me any more. You're twenty. It's high time you stood on your own two feet."

"But you promised Daddy," she wailed. "On his deathbed you promised him that you would take care of me."

"And I have." Not for the fist time Erin wished that she had never told Crystal about her promise to her father four years ago. Struck down with pancreatic cancer, his death had been sudden. She'd taken six months away from the last module of her chef's training to take care of him, but that had been overly optimistic. He'd died two months after being diagnosed.

Crystal changed tactics. "It's about Dominic, isn't it? You're still mad about that, aren't you?"

"Who, me?" Erin raised an eyebrow. "Mad because I found my sister making out with the only man who's been interested me in years? Why should I be mad about that?"

"But you weren't really serious about him were you?" Crystal took a step backward, a look of genuine surprise on her face. "I mean, you didn't even try to get him back."

Erin stared at her sister as though seeing her for the first time. Where had she gone wrong? Images, memories, sensations from the past tumbled through her mind like balls in a lotto machine, but this was no time to start wondering what she might have done differently. Besides, there would be plenty of time for reflection in the next few days.

"Be that as it may, I never thanked you properly."

"Thanked me?" Crystal's hand fluttered at her neck. "What for?"

"For showing me what Dominic was really like before I got any more involved." Erin forced a smile onto her lips. "So thanks."

"Oh. Well. You're welcome. I guess." Crystal looked confused.

Erin softened her voice. "Dominic doesn't matter, Crys. What matters is that you're finally going to learn to be on your own. I probably should have asked you to take on more responsibility, but we can't undo that now. It's going to be fun, you'll see." Crystal shrugged and looked away, her typical reaction when she didn't want to discuss something. "Besides, we've been talking about this for the last year or so. You're the one who brought it up, and you were right. You need to be in charge of your own life. You have a job, the house is paid for, and I've left you enough money to pay the utilities and upkeep for three months."

"But I want you to do it. I don't want you to go."

Erin shook her head. "Of course you don't. But that's only because you want me here to do things for you, like make sure the bills get paid and cook and clean. But let's face it, when it comes to your social life, you've been doing your own thing for the past couple of years now. I've practically had to make an appointment to see you." She became suddenly businesslike. "Speaking of which, I'll call you as soon as I get to The Lodge. Let you know I arrived safely. I left the phone number on the kitchen counter."

Crystal turned away. "Don't bother."

Now she's going to sulk, thought Erin. But this time I'm not going to try to pull her out of it. She wanted to pump her fist in the air. It was about time she stood up for herself. Her sister's wants and needs had taken precedence for too long, but that was going to change as of right now. She glanced at her reflection in the ornate hall mirror then paused for a closer inspection. She didn't look anything like her gorgeous sister. Crystal was slender, blond, and supremely self-confident. Standing beside her, Erin often felt like somebody's kid brother. Okay, so that was a bit of an exaggeration, but the thought always helped her over the awkwardness of being compared to her sister. Made her forget that men always looked at Crystal first. Always had, always would, she supposed. With a flash of insight she realized that her lack of self-esteem and her inability to stand up to her sister's constant demands were somehow connected.

"You don't mean that. I'll call you when I arrive."

Crystal turned on her, pale blue eyes as cold as ice.

"I'm serious. Two can play this game, you know. If you want to go running off to some stupid fishing lodge, then go ahead, but don't call me and whine about how remote it is, or how the kitchen isn't properly equipped. Personally I think you're crazy." She shot a sly look at her sister. "Dominic thinks so too. I mean, you only met the owner once, and based on that you're going off to the middle of nowhere to be his chef?"

Erin gave her head a quick shake. It was evident that her sister hadn't cared enough to listen when she'd told her about checking out her new employer and his exclusive operation. The major shareholder in one of the largest logging companies in British Columbia, David Kendall had built the finest fishing lodge on the West Coast. Known simply as 'The Lodge' to its guests, the floating facility was completely self-sufficient, and could be moved from site to site depending on how the fish were running. Right now it was anchored in one of the innumerable inlets that make up the coastline of British Columbia.

"I'm sorry you feel that way." A horn sounded outside, and Erin looked through the glass in the front door. "There's my taxi."

"That's another thing," continued her sister. "If this is such a high class place, why don't they fly you up like their customers? Why do you have to take the bus all the way to Port Hardy and leave from there on some stupid boat?" She crossed her arms as though she had scored a major point.

Erin sighed. "Because I have two weeks free before I start work and because I choose to do it this way.

Granted, spending an entire day on the bus and overnight at the hotel isn't too thrilling, but a leisurely boat trip up to The Lodge will make up for it." The horn sounded again, and she gave her unresponsive sister a quick hug. Picking up her duffel bag, she ran quickly down the steps and climbed into the taxi, tears stinging the back of her eyes. "Bus station," she said firmly. She was doing the right thing. She knew it as surely as she'd known anything in her life. Settling back in her seat, she hoped she wouldn't regret her decision to travel by boat. She'd find out soon enough tomorrow.

Chapter One

Erin stood at the top of the ramp, surveying the marina. She'd been awake for several hours already—anxious but excited at the prospect of the boat trip. The security gate was open, but she could see no movement below, where sleek sailboats vied for space with cabin cruisers and more modest watercraft. The only sound was the soft clink of rigging against a metal mast. A few wispy remnants of early morning mist danced over the water, dissipating quickly as the rising sun burned them off.

The quiet was broken by the raucous call of a seagull. She watched it fly a short distance to the shoreline, where it attacked a cluster of exposed mollusks. Steadying herself with one hand on the railing, she stepped onto the ramp, which was tilted at a steep angle by the low tide. Thankful that she'd thought to wear sneakers, she made her way cautiously down toward water level.

Safely on the dock, she adjusted her duffel bag over her shoulder and sauntered toward the larger boats at the far end of the marina. "It's a converted fishing trawler," she'd been told on the phone. "You'll find it moored near the other fishing boats. Look for a sign that says *Legend.*"

A sign nailed to a piling at the second to last slip pointed her toward a sturdy white boat with blue trim. Coming to a stop beside a pile of wooden crates she looked around for signs of life. Shading her eyes from the sun, she looked into the wheelhouse. It seemed deserted, but then she was more than half an hour early. Testing the strength of the crates, she sat on the largest one, content to listen to the slap of the water on the bottom of the dock.

"Hey you!" A head popped up from somewhere below. "Those crates aren't for sitting on." Dark-blue eyes in an unshaven face regarded her coolly. Gray-flecked hair showed below a short black woolen cap.

She leaped to her feet. This couldn't be the captain, she decided. He must be a deckhand, and he was unbelievably rude. "Well excuse me," she said, surprising herself with the forcefulness of her words, "but they're quite strong, I assure you." She slapped the wood with her hand, trying not to wince as a sliver pierced her palm.

He grunted, turned his back, and disappeared below decks. Erin stared after him, angered by his behavior. David Kendall had recommended *Legend* and she made a mental note to have a word with him when she got to The Lodge.

She took a few steps along the dock, examining the boat with a critical eye. It gleamed with a new coat of paint, and the metal surfaces shone impressively. If those things were anything to go by, at least the transportation was sound.

"Are you still here?" The man had re-appeared silently and was standing on the deck of the boat, legs widespread. There was something about him that didn't fit with her idea of a deckhand, but then what did she know? He was dressed simply in a dark blue T-shirt that echoed the color of his eyes, and his legs were encased in faded denims. Over the T-shirt, he wore a leather jacket that looked so soft she wanted to reach out and touch it.

She glared at him. "Of course I'm still here. I'm looking for Ben."

"Ben's not here. Broke his leg."

"But that can't be," she cried out. "He's supposed to take me to The Lodge."

"I don't think so." He stepped onto the dock, ignoring her.

"Now wait just a minute!" She couldn't believe she was confronting him, but it felt good. She should stand up for herself more often. "I don't know who you are, but I spoke with David Kendall a few days ago and he assured me that this boat—" she pointed to the name on the bow "*Legend*, was leaving from Port Hardy this morning and that I could travel on it."

"Who?" He was examining the crates.

"My new employer, David Kendall. He hired me personally and he owns The Lodge." She jabbed a finger at the boat. "For all I know, he owns this boat too."

"No way, lady. *Legend* belongs to my friend Ben." He effortlessly picked up one of the crates and took it on board. "And while he's laid up, I'm filling in for him. I have two passengers and they're both men. One's a guest and the other's the new chef." He set down the crate and pulled a folded-up piece of paper out of his pocket, flicking it with a finger. "Says so right here. Two passengers. William Corbett and Aaron Delaney." He grinned at her, enjoying his role as bearer of bad news. "I guess that leaves you out."

"Guess again." She leaned back against the crates, giving him her sweetest smile. "I'm the new chef. My name's Erin Delaney."

To his credit, he didn't miss a beat, but a flash of anger altered his features for a moment, then disappeared. "Figures," he said shortly, then continued loading. "Didn't you bring a bag or anything?"

"Back there." She gestured behind the crates on the dock. "Mr. Kendall arranged for most of my things to be shipped up. I just brought a couple of changes of clothes and some silly gifts I got at a going away party." She didn't know why she was suddenly babbling. "But that's probably more information than you need, huh?"

He ignored her feeble attempt at humor. "If you're waiting for me to carry your bag, you'll wait a long time. This is definitely a no-frills cruise."

"That much is obvious," she muttered, picking up her duffel bag.

"It's not too late," he said hopefully. "You could always fly up, you know." He was back on the dock now, hoisting another crate.

She dropped her bag. "You'd like that, wouldn't you? Well read my lips, buster. I spent over ten hours in a bus yesterday so I could be on this boat and I'm not going back now." She clenched her hands at her sides, and the sliver bit into her flesh. She blinked rapidly, ignoring the pain. "What's your name, anyway?"

He turned to face her. "Why? Are you going to report me to the famous Mr. Kendall?"

"Why do I get the feeling you'd like that?" she challenged.

"Gray."

"I beg your pardon?"

"Gray. It's short for Graydon, although I must confess I was getting to like 'buster'.

"Very funny." She picked up her bag and followed him onto the boat. "You can call me Erin."

"Well, Erin." He hiked his head toward a set of narrow steps. "Stow your stuff down below. Grab any bunk you like. It's just the three of us."

She descended a steep stairway and looked around in amazement. All of the woodwork was polished teak with gleaming brass accents. A compact, well-equipped galley hugged one bulkhead, leaving ample room opposite for what looked like a restaurant booth. Further inspection revealed two cozy bunks in the forward section, with two more aft of the dining area. Not an inch of space was wasted, but instead of feeling claustrophobic, the living quarters were warm and inviting. She poked her head inside the bathroom, surprised to find it larger than she had anticipated. "Head" she said aloud. "If I call it the bathroom, he'll never let me live it down." Delighted with the interior, she tossed her bag on one of the forward bunks and went back up the stairway.

Gray had brought the last crates aboard and was securing them to the back deck. His jacket lay on the steps leading into the wheelhouse and she watched silently as broad shoulders flexed beneath the T-shirt. Tying off a rope, he stood back to survey his work with a look of satisfaction. He glanced up to see her watching him, and for a fleeting moment she wished that they could start all over again. She turned and looked away from the marina—anything to avoid those piercing eyes. A seal surfaced beside the boat and she turned to him, eager to share the experience, but he wasn't there. He was on the dock, walking toward an older man, hand outstretched. So, she thought, he can be gracious when he chooses. She hated to admit it, but it rankled that he'd been so curt with her. And yes, she was angry with herself for being sharp in return. Taking control of her life was all well and good, but surely it could be done without over-reacting every time she met some handsome guy with a chip on his shoulder. She tilted her head, watching him speaking with the older man. No way was she going to let him ruin the trip. She could easily put up with him for the two nights it took to get to The Lodge. After all, this was her first free time in several years. She intended to enjoy it.

"Hi Bill." Gray stuck out his hand. "How are you feeling?"

"Quite well, considering." The older man shook hands, a broad smile on his face. "I didn't expect to see you here." He glanced over Gray's shoulder. "Where's Ben?"

"He broke his leg, and I'm filling in for him. He's just beginning to get his feet on the ground financially. Can't afford to lose any of his contracts. Several of us who know how to operate the boat are going to cover for him until he can come back."

The older man nodded knowingly. "Good. I'd hate to see him lose everything he's worked for." His gaze returned to the boat. "I see your other passenger showed up."

"The new chef, no less. Hired personally by the great David Kendall. Probably one of his conquests." Gray's tone was bitter. "She even had the gall to suggest that he owns the boat."

"Come on, son. That's not fair either to David or to her. I spoke to him just the other day and she's evidently a terrific chef. Besides,"—he lowered his voice a notch—"she's not quite his type. He's partial to blondes."

Gray nodded slowly. That let Erin off the hook. When she'd turned away he couldn't help noticing the way her hair gleamed in the morning sun. It reminded him of the rich colors of the copper beech trees that lined the street where he'd grown up. "I suppose you're right," he agreed reluctantly. "But she sure is a pain."

Bill smiled knowingly. "Told you off, did she?"

"Not on her best day." Gray picked up Bill's suitcase, then turned with a half smile. "Well, maybe a little. Come on, let's get you on board and settled."

Erin watched the exchange with interest. The two men obviously knew each other, entering into a lively exchange. She shrugged off the notion that they were talking about her.

The new arrival stepped onto the boat and looked around appreciatively. Erin estimated him to be somewhere around sixty. He smiled in her direction and crossed the deck, offering his hand.

"Delighted to meet you," he said in a deep, raspy voice. "Bill Corbett. Gray tells me you're the new chef at The Lodge."

"Yes, that's right. I'm Erin Delaney."

"Excellent." He turned his face to the sun. "Looks like it's going to be a nice day. I've been looking forward to this trip for several weeks." He braced himself against the railing and exhaled slowly.

"Me too." In the harsh light of the sun she noticed the unhealthy pallor of the man's skin, and the dark smudges around his eyes. She opened her mouth to speak, but was distracted by a woman's voice on the dock. Out of breath and excited, it sounded like Crystal. Erin's stomach plunged.

"Am I too late?" The woman stood on the dock, teetering on high-heeled sandals that were tied around her ankles with grosgrain ribbon. Large designer sunglasses hid her eyes and blond hair almost the exact color and length of Crystal's flowed down her back. Weak with relief, Erin realized it was not her sister.

Gray exploded out of the wheelhouse, feet barely touching the steps as he came down onto the deck. "Too late for what?" he said, sounding surprisingly human.

"This is *Legend,* isn't it?" The woman removed her sunglasses, revealing startling blue eyes.

Gray nodded.

"Oh good. Then I'm not too late. I was told that you have room for one more passenger." She smiled up at him. "You must be Ben."

Erin wondered what it must be like to have men fall at your feet. Well okay, Gray wasn't exactly falling at the woman's feet, but he wasn't yelling at her either. An unexpected stab of jealousy brought her up short.

"No, Ma'am." He stepped down onto the dock. "Ben had an accident. I don't know who you were talking to but . . ."

"Oh please." She laid a hand on his arm. "I want to surprise my husband. He's at The Lodge. I know I could fly, but somebody told me that they post a list of new arrivals every day and I don't want him to see my name." She stopped abruptly, eyes wide. "You do still have space, don't you?"

"Well yes, but . . ."

"Thank goodness." Erin saw tears well up in the woman's eyes and turned away. How many times had Crystal used exactly the same tactics? "You don't know how much this means to me."

Bill Corbett was watching the exchange with interest, a faint smile on his face. Gray looked helplessly in his direction.

Bill shrugged. "Give the lady a break, Gray. There's room for one more."

The woman stuck out her hand and Erin noticed it was trembling slightly. "Angela Siebring. I promise I won't be any bother."

Gray took the proffered hand, shaking it briskly.

"Okay, but you're going to have to change your shoes."
He pointed at her feet. "You won't last five minutes in
those things. Do you have anything else?"

"I'll go barefoot if necessary, but I think I can find
something." She held up an overnight bag. "I'm travelling light, as you can see."

"Well get down below and claim a bunk and change
those shoes. Erin can show you around."

Erin bristled, but thought better of clashing with
Gray again. "Down there," she said, pointing toward
the stairwell. "I'll be right behind you."

She turned to Gray. "Is there something we can sit on
out here? Folding chairs or something like that?" She
didn't care so much for herself, but Bill Corbett looked
as though a good stiff wind would blow him over.

"I know Ben's got some around her somewhere." He
walked to a door beneath the wheelhouse and Erin followed. Collapsible canvas chairs leaned against one
side of a small locker, and above them life vests hung
on hooks. As Gray hauled out four of the chairs, Erin
spotted a fire extinguisher mounted on the back of the
door. She smiled to herself. Noting the position of fire
extinguishers was second nature to anyone who worked
in a kitchen for very long.

The older man eased himself into a chair with a
grateful sigh and Erin picked up his suitcase. "Shall I
take this below for you, Mr. Corbett? Seems like I've
been elected to show Angela around."

Eyes that were somewhere between gray and green
regarded her kindly. "I'd appreciate that, Erin. And call
me Bill."

"I'll do that. And when I get back, I'll bring you a cup of coffee." She turned to Gray. "If that's okay with you."

"Whatever. I'm sure you can find what you need. As for me, I need to get underway."

At the bottom on the stairs, Erin was greeted by silence. Angela's bag was on the unclaimed forward bunk, contents strewn around, but there was no sign of the blond. A muffled sound came from the head, and Erin relaxed, deciding to use the time to inspect the galley. Cookware, cutlery, dishes and food supplies were all secured against the motion of the ship. Quickly and efficiently, she put on a pot of coffee and sat down to wait.

Moments later the door to the head opened and Angela emerged, smiling brightly—too brightly. Nothing could hide the fact that she'd been crying. An expert at tears, Erin recognized the real thing. She tried not to stare at the other woman, but it was difficult to avoid the obvious in such close quarters. Here was another woman as opposite from herself in looks and temperament as it was possible to get. She was tall, thin, beautiful and, if her earlier performance was to be believed, rather ditsy. Erin wanted to dislike her, yet she found herself sympathizing with the other woman.

"Did you find any shoes to wear?" Erin looked down at Angela's feet. Even her feet were beautiful, the toenails gleaming with soft peach polish.

Angela dabbed at her eyes with a handful of tissue and gestured toward the disaster on her bunk. "I've got some sneakers in there somewhere." A fresh torrent of tears ran silently down her cheeks. "I'm sorry but I'm not very good company right now. You don't really need to show me around, you know." A deep, throaty rumble indicated that they were underway.

"All right. That's my bag on the bunk opposite yours, so it looks like the sleeping arrangements will work out. As for showing you around, what you see is what you get." She took down two coffee mugs. "I promised Bill I'd take him some coffee. Help yourself and come on up on deck when you feel up to it. Gray dug out some chairs, so at least there's a spot for us to sit."

Angela nodded and turned away, leaving Erin to pour the coffee and load her pocket with packets of sugar and individual creamers.

"Here we are," she said, emerging onto the deck. They were moving slowly, still inside the breakwater of the marina. Bill had positioned a chair beside one of the crates, and Erin set the mugs down then emptied her pocket. "All the comforts of home."

"Thanks, Erin." Bill reached for two packets of sugar. "I limit myself to two cups a day, and I haven't had one yet, so this is going to taste good." He stirred the steaming liquid slowly with a spoon that she produced with a flourish. "You know, I've never seen the coast this way. I've flown up many times, but you don't really get to see anything." He picked up the mug, cradling it between both hands and blowing on the surface of the liquid. "As I said before, I've been looking forward to this."

Erin pulled a chair closer and dumped two creams into her coffee. "To tell you the truth, I thought I'd be the only passenger. I had no idea the trip would appeal to anyone else."

"Funny you should say that. I too thought I'd be the only one on board." He saluted her with the mug. "But I'm delighted to have some company."

"Good." She studied the older man. "But don't worry, I won't talk your ear off."

He raised the mug to his lips then lowered it again without drinking. "I believe you." Weary eyes studied her. "In my experience there are two kinds of women. Women of action, and women who rely on words. You appear to be one of the former."

"Gee." Erin gave a short, nervous laugh. "I'm not sure if I'm flattered, but you're right." She tilted her head to one side. "Are you a people watcher?"

Bill nodded. "I think I've always been an observer of human nature." He returned her gaze. "How about you?"

"I'm more of a caretaker, I suppose. I brought up my younger sister and too often I found myself putting her needs before my own." She held up a hand as though to ward off a comment. "Not to sound noble or anything. It's just the way I am." She plunged ahead. "Speaking of caretaking, you look awfully tired."

A gentle smile tugged at the corner of his mouth and his gaze drifted out over the waters of Queen Charlotte Strait. "I'm healthier today than I've been for some time, even though it might not look that way. I had open heart surgery recently, so if I look tired and pale, that's the reason." He took a long, slow sip of coffee, closing his eyes in appreciation. "My voice isn't always scratchy like this, but they have to shove a tube down your throat for something like that, and it's only now starting to heal." He gave her a blissful smile. "It's true what they say, you know. A near brush with death makes you see things differently. All of a sudden it wasn't important to get to The Lodge in a hurry. Besides, my doctor tells me that fresh air and a nice, slow trip will do me good."

Erin nodded. "Did you mention a special diet when you called to reserve the boat? I'm quite sure it won't be any problem at The Lodge."

He waved away her concerns. "No need. I don't eat a lot, and I'll be careful. But thank you for asking. No, I think the best medicine for me right now is to sit right here and watch the scenery go by. I'm hoping to see some Orcas, and when we get across the strait and start our run up the coast of the mainland there should be lots of other wildlife."

They skirted an island and were soon out in the channel separating Vancouver Island from the mainland. The sea was unusually calm, and the powerful motors cut through the water effortlessly, leaving behind a churning wake.

"How long do you think it'll take us to get over to the mainland?" Erin stood up and leaned on the railing, breathing in the tangy sea air.

"I'm no expert, but the motors sound powerful. "I'd guess we'll be on the far side in the early afternoon." He stretched out his feet and his entire body seemed to relax. "Frankly I don't care if it takes all day." He cocked his head, looking up at her. "Are you on a tight schedule? You young people always seem to be running somewhere these days."

"Multi-tasking," said Erin with a wry grin. "One of those words that didn't even exist when you were younger."

"Bingo. My theory is that most of this frantic behavior is due to the proliferation of cell phones." He gave his head a quick shake. "Don't let me get started on that. I'm one of the few people I know who don't have a cell phone."

"Well you can add me to the list. I had one but it was a nuisance." Erin removed the clip that held her long hair in a twist at the back of her head. Hair streaming out behind her, she lifted her face to the sun. "But to answer your question, I'm not on any schedule at the moment. My job at The Lodge doesn't start for two weeks, but I'd already said good-bye to everyone at the restaurant where I worked, and Mr. Kendall told me I could arrive any time, so here I am." She opened her eyes and glanced toward the wheelhouse. "The only fly in the ointment is our captain. I'm afraid we didn't get off to a very good start."

"That's too bad." Bill drained the coffee mug. "Maybe some of this excellent coffee would help to patch things up."

Erin's palms turned clammy and she brushed them on her slacks, irritating the sliver again. She examined her hand, noting that the sliver had worked its way beneath the skin. It would fester if she didn't get it out soon.

Bill was still enjoying the spectacular scenery and

hadn't noticed her distress. "What do you say—time to bury the hatchet, isn't it?"

"I suppose so, but it feels like being with Crystal all over again." The older man looked at her curiously, his quiet, non-judgmental demeanor inviting confidence.

"Sorry," she said. "Crystal is my sister's name and for the last four years it's been just the two of us." She pressed the fingers of her right hand into her temple, as though trying to suppress the memories. "In my role of caretaker I always ended up apologizing just to keep the peace."

Setting his mug on the nearest crate Bill rose and came to stand beside her. "I imagine that was difficult for you, but that man up there . . ." he angled his head toward the wheelhouse, "is not your sister."

She nodded silently. A seagull rode the air currents over the strait, eyeing the two figures expectantly. When no food was forthcoming it sheared away, continuing its quest. Finally Erin met his eyes. "You're right, of course." Before he could respond she gave him a quick kiss on the cheek, picked up the two empty coffee mugs and went below.

Angela was sitting at the table, slender fingers playing with a glass of water. She looked up as Erin entered the cabin. "I guess I should go up there and be sociable, huh?" Lifting the glass, she took a sip, watching Erin over the rim.

"Only if you want to." Erin placed the dirty mugs in the sink and took out a clean one. "I'm going back up now."

"I'll wash those mugs for you and put them away."

Erin whirled on the other woman. "Why—"

Angela stood up quickly. "I didn't mean to sound critical. It's just that my husband has a boat and I've learned to stow everything away the minute we're finished with it." She waggled her hand back and forth. "Things tend to slide around in big seas." She moved to the small sink and ran the cups under the hot water. "You know, your hair is gorgeous like that. You should wear it down all the time."

"Oh, no, I couldn't do that." Heat crept up Erin's neck and into her face. It was a long time since she'd blushed, but then it was also a long time since anyone had paid her a compliment. She fumbled in her pocket for the hair clip and secured her hair at the back of her neck.

"Why ever not?" Angela lifted the heavy mass that lay against Erin's back, letting it fall through her fingers. "I'll bet your boyfriend likes it down."

Dominic's face swam before her eyes, followed closely by the painful image of his arms wrapped around Crystal. "I wouldn't know," she said abruptly, pouring coffee. "I don't have a boyfriend. Now I really should get this up to Gray." She fled up the stairs.

Chapter Two

T wo steps led up to the wheelhouse. Erin took a deep breath, suddenly apprehensive. It was hard to understand why Gray had taken such an instant dislike to her. She couldn't remember ever clashing like this with anyone before. Except that sous-chef she'd worked with at the restaurant. But then, he hated everyone.

Gray beckoned her inside. "Come on, I won't bite."

She set the mug down and managed a grin. "You just want this coffee." She patted her pockets. "I still have some cream and some sugar, but something tells me you take it black."

He raised his eyebrows. "Black and hot." His eyes were constantly in motion, checking the gauges displayed before him, scanning the water ahead. He gestured to a tall stool, much like the one he occupied. "Make yourself comfortable."

She hated to appear clumsy, but managed to ease up

24

onto the stool with a minimum of effort. It was surprising how the few extra feet of height in the wheelhouse translated into a much better view of the surrounding ocean. "Bill and I were wondering how long until we reach the mainland."

"In a hurry?"

His voice teased and she gave him a sharp, questioning look. Was this the same man who had greeted her earlier? "Not really," she said slowly. "As a matter of fact we were talking about how we're absolutely not in a hurry."

"Were you now." He unrolled a large laminated chart, the edges curled and frayed from use. "This is our present position," he said, tracing a dotted line with a finger. "And we should be over here by late this afternoon. We're on a northeasterly heading."

"Wow. Look at all those islands—and those inlets. It's like a maze." Erin leaned over the map but she was having a difficult time concentrating. She hadn't expected him to smell so good. The effect was dizzying. She pulled back and found him watching her carefully.

"Something the matter?" A frown pulled his eyebrows together.

"Uh, no." Confused by her reaction, she turned away. The boat rode over a swell and she braced herself against the doorjamb, then pulled her hand away quickly, as though she'd been burned.

"How's that hand?"

"My hand?" She looked at is as though it belonged to someone else.

"Yeah, the splinter. Here, let me have a look."

He held out his hand and she placed hers in it. His skin was surprisingly smooth for someone who worked on a boat, but that fact barely registered. Her heart was hammering against her ribs. "How did you know?"

He frowned. "I saw you wince when you slammed your hand down on the crate this morning. It's been bothering you ever since." His eyes sparkled with amusement. "Temper, temper."

She tried to pull back but he held on firmly. "Listen," he said quietly. "This has to come out. I can't do anything while we're underway, but I'll take it out tonight. Is that okay?"

She nodded, wondering what had happened to her voice.

"Good." He picked up the mug and took a long gulp. "I'll see you later then."

She stumbled back onto the deck, surprised to see that Angela was sitting quietly beside Bill. She started to rise but Erin waved her down, pulling one of the folded chairs from behind a crate and sitting down with her back to the wheelhouse. Those blue eyes saw too much. She wasn't about to reveal any more of herself than absolutely necessary.

"So. I saw you chatting with Gray," said Bill casually. "Did you ask him when we'd reach the mainland?"

Erin silently thanked him for not referring to their earlier conversation. "I did as a matter of fact. He says we're heading northeast, and that we'll be off the coast by late this afternoon."

Bill studied the sky. "With this weather I'll bet he wants to run late this evening. It will be light 'til at least ten o'clock and tomorrow's weather looks iffy. I checked early this morning."

"Aren't you clever." Angela's remark sounded fatuous, but Erin could see that she was sincere. The woman was an enigma.

"Do I know you?" Bill was studying the blond with clinical detachment. "I swear I know your face from somewhere."

Angela endured his scrutiny with patient dignity. "You might have seen my face during my career as a model. I haven't work for several years now, but I did a lot of print ads during my day. You know the sort—newspapers, flyers, magazines. Even those big ads on the sides of buses a few times." She shrugged. "I was never what you call famous, though."

Bill nodded vigorously. "That's it. I must have seen you in my . . ." He hesitated. "In the newspaper."

"And what type of business are you in, Mr. Corbett?"

"I'm retired now. But I was in communications."

"Thank goodness my husband isn't here," she said, leaning toward the older man. "Daniel lost a lot of money in the dot com bust and he hasn't stopped talking about it since. He won't admit it, but the fact is he had too much exposure to communications stocks although his losses were more than offset by some pretty phenomenal gains, so he can't really complain." She paused, then continued with a sigh. "But he still does."

"Thanks for the warning. I'll be sure to steer well away from that subject if I encounter him at The Lodge." Bill laced his fingers over his stomach and leaned back, closing his eyes.

Erin stood up and wandered over to the rail. Vancouver Island was becoming fuzzy around the edges as they left it behind. The distant mountains folded into each other, fading from dark green to soft purplish grey in the distance. It was becoming difficult to distinguish where the tip of the island ended and the sea began. Leaning on the railing, she stared down into the water. It was hard to believe that there had been a time—was that only a few weeks ago?—when she'd been drowning in a pool of self-pity, wondering how she would ever pull herself out. And then she'd met David Kendall at The Round House.

It had been a busy night and the kitchen had produced a record number of meals. Just to complicate things, the owner had arrived unannounced, apologetic but expecting them to rearrange seating to accommodate his party of four. As usual, the staff had handled the disruption with quiet efficiency. She'd been drinking a cup of her preferred green tea after the crush was over when a tall man with pure white hair walked into her kitchen. She instinctively moved to meet him—but not for the reason he thought. "Customers aren't allowed in here," she informed him. "I'm sorry, but I'll have to ask you to leave."

"I understand," he said graciously. "Frank said you'd probably kick me out, but I just had to come and meet the person who coordinates all this." He waved a hand. "I must say, you do a remarkable job. Our meals were sublime."

"Frank Williams?"

"Yes. He's an old friend of mine. Which is why I

gave him fair warning that I intend to steal you away from him." He smiled and extended his hand. "David Kendall. Have you heard of the Pacific Coast Lodge? Most folks just call it The Lodge."

"I can't say I have." She set down the tea and shook his hand. "Are you serious, Mr. Kendall?"

"Absolutely." His eyes sparkled, and Erin decided that he was probably the most self-confident man she'd ever met. "I want you to come and be my chef."

She didn't quite know how to handle this frontal attack other than to be blunt right back. "Do you always get what you want, Mr. Kendall?"

He hesitated for a moment. "Not always, but if I really want something I go after it. Call me David."

"Well David, I admire the direct approach, but I'm quite happy right here."

"Frank told me you'd say that as well." Reaching into his jacket he extracted a slim billfold, and handed her his card. "I know you can't talk right now, but I'll be in touch."

"But I'm serious," she said, tucking the card in her pocket without a glance.

"So am I Erin. So am I." And he'd walked out.

The offer had come formally, in a letter. It felt good to be wanted, and the dollar figure was surprisingly generous. But what had surprised her even more was Frank's reaction. The restaurant owner made it clear that there would be no hard feelings if she took the position. "If I were you, I'd take him up on it," he'd said over coffee one night.

"Are you trying to get rid of me?" she'd asked with a

sly smile. It was a blatant demand for a compliment, and he didn't disappoint.

"Of course not—you know better than that. You're the best chef I've ever had. It's just that offers like this don't come along very often."

"And so here I am," she said aloud, returning to the present.

"Did you say something?" Angela appeared at her side. "You looked like you were deep in thought. I wasn't sure if I should disturb you."

"I was just thinking about leaving the restaurant where I worked for several years and hoping I'm making a wise move." Erin looked at the beautiful woman at her side. "I know my business inside and out but when it comes to my personal life I'm not quite as confident as you are."

Angela flattened a hand on her chest. "Me? Confident? Now that's a laugh." A few strands of blond hair streamed across her face and she tucked it impatiently behind her ear. "I'm so nervous about going up to The Lodge. I'm not sure what sort of a reception I'll get from Daniel."

"Your husband, right?"

Angela's face softened. "Yeah. He's a great guy, but we had a terrible row before he left. That's why I was making a fool of myself earlier."

"You don't need to explain that."

"Maybe not, but I do want to apologize. I can't imagine what you must think of me."

"Oh that's easy." Erin gave a short laugh. "You're gorgeous."

The other woman brushed aside the compliment with a flick of the hand. "On the outside maybe. But inside I'm a mess." Eyes brimming with tears she turned and looked at Erin. "I actually shouted at him. I told him to just go away, and he did."

"But you know where he is at least." Unaccustomed to receiving confidences, Erin couldn't think of anything else to say.

"Yes. I suppose I should be grateful for that. I wouldn't answer the phone so he left a message telling me where he is. Now I only hope he'll forgive me."

Erin smiled into the other woman's eyes. "He'll forgive you. I can feel it in my bones."

"I hope you're right." She copied Erin's pose, leaning on the railing and looking down into the dark green water. "That was nice what you said about me, but you don't have any reason to be jealous, you know."

"Oh no?" Erin eyed her skeptically. "Tell you what. Let's trade bodies for a couple of weeks. Then we'll see if you still feel the same way."

Angela refused to back off. "But you've got so much going for you. You're a take charge kind of person. I can tell that even though I've only known you a couple of hours. And you're off to a new job at the most exclusive resort on the West Coast. How can you miss?"

"Do you hear yourself? Those things are about my career. They're not about the way I look. You of all people should know that thin is in, being a former model and all. I'm overweight. It's as simple as that."

"That's where you're wrong! It's anything but simple." Angela pulled back, anger clouding her eyes.

"How can we educate our young girls if people our age are still buying into the idea that they have to be able to fit into the smallest clothes in the store. You're not overweight."

Erin struggled not to lose her temper. "Next to you I am."

Angela gave her a critical once-over. "All right, you weigh more than I do, but you're not what I'd call seriously overweight." She laid a slender hand on Erin's forearm. "I speak to hundreds of young girls every year about the importance of self-image. I warn them against the dangers of anorexia. It's a serious problem." She stopped to catch her breath, eyes blazing with intensity. "Look at you. You've got great skin and terrific hair. You're far from being fat. Please believe me about this."

Erin was suddenly very interested in a passing freighter.

"So?" Angela's usually breathy voice was surprisingly insistent. "What do you say?"

Erin wanted to believe her, but she'd been comparing herself to Crystal for too many years. It would take more than a few words from Angela to change her mind. How could she be so confident in her work and so insecure about her personal life? She pushed away from the railing and smiled at the other woman. "I know you mean well, but this would be a major attitude change for me. In the meantime I'm going to see about lunch."

The stairs leading down to the cabin were blurry, but Erin managed to navigate them without falling down.

Chest heaving, she stood in the small galley, forcing back the tears. Why had she let Angela's remarks get to her? Slumping onto the bench beside the table she braced her head in her hands. Angela had given her a lot to think about, but how could someone who looked like that even begin know how she felt? She doubted that the former model had ever been anything but slim and gorgeous.

"Erin?" Angela stood at the foot of the stairs, one hand on the railing as though prepared to dash back up in a hurry. "I'm sorry if I spoke out of turn."

Erin's anger dissolved. "What was that Jack Nicholson line in that movie?" she asked wearily.

"Which one?"

"The one where he said something about not being able to handle the truth."

Angela placed both hands on her hips and puffed out her lips. "*You can't handle the truth!*" she shouted, doing a fair imitation of the famous movie star.

Erin collapsed on the bench in a fit of laughter. "That was fantastic!" She dabbed at her eyes. "Has anyone ever told you you're hilarious?"

"No." Angela's lips twitched, and a slow smile spread over her face. "No, they haven't." She leaned against the counter. "Does this mean you're not mad at me any more?"

Erin waved a hand in front of her face. "I was never mad at you. Listen, do me a favor, will you? Go up and ask Gray what he had planned for lunch, or if we should just wing it. I don't want anybody to see my red eyes."

"Gladly."

While Angela was gone she did a quick inventory of the food. A small well-stocked freezer held enough supplies for a week of meals.

"I talked to Gray." Angela had returned from her visit to the wheelhouse. "He says he was going to suggest sandwiches, but that it's up to us." She hesitated. "I got the impression that he didn't want you to think he expected you to cook just because you're a chef."

"Really?" Erin tried to sound casual.

"Yeah. As a matter of fact, those were his exact words."

Smiling to herself, Erin started to pull items from the refrigerator. "The truth is, I'm not used to sitting around, so I'd be happy to do the cooking." She paused. "That is if it's okay with you."

"Only if I can help out and do the washing up."

"It's a deal." She placed a chopping board, sharp knife and some onions in front of the other woman. "Chop up these onions really fine." Erin glared at the former model, but there was an underlying warmth in her eyes. "I'm going to fatten you up with some bruschetta and soup."

Erin delivered a mug of soup and several large slices of bruschetta to the wheelhouse. Gray looked dubiously at the bruschetta, then devoured the first crispy slice in several bites, groaning with pleasure. "Bill and Angela are eating down below," she said as he reached for the mug. "I think Bill would have preferred to eat outside, but with the soup and all . . ." she eased up onto the empty stool, her back to the corner.

"When Ben is running up the coast he usually stops for meals. At least he did the time I went with him. There are so many secluded bays and islands you could stop in a different spot every time and never run out of new ones." He made a small course correction.

"So this isn't your regular job?" Her eyes touched on all the electronics. "You seem to know what you're doing."

"I wouldn't be here if I didn't. Even I'm not that foolish."

"Are you avoiding my question?"

"Kinda nosy, aren't you." It was more of a statement than a question.

"Well, that answers that."

"Excuse me?" He paused, a slice of bruschetta halfway to his mouth.

"For a while there, I thought maybe we'd get along. But I can see that isn't going to happen." She slid down off the stool. "I'm going to make some stew and biscuits for dinner, so you can eat any time you're hungry." She gestured toward the dishes. "Angela will come up for those later."

"I'm a pilot."

"A pilot?" One foot on the step, she turned and looked at him.

"Yeah. A pilot."

"An airline pilot?" She couldn't quite picture him walking through an airport in a crisp uniform, trailing one of those square suitcases. Or was that the flight attendants?

"In a way." He slipped on a pair of dark sunglasses,

as if to confirm the image. "If one aircraft can be called an airline. I do charters, flying fishermen into remote locations along the coast."

Erin nodded knowingly. "Including The Lodge, I suppose."

"Including The Lodge."

"So who's minding the store while you're here?" She took a step back into the wheelhouse.

"I rebooked the reservations I'd accepted with someone else, and I've left a message on my website and on my answering machine. I have a friend who can take over in a pinch if anything new comes up."

Erin looked beyond the windows of the wheelhouse. The mainland was coming up quickly. At least she thought it was the mainland. From a distance, the islands and inlets that made up the coast folded together, making it difficult to distinguish one piece of land from the other. "So this is a different perspective for you. You're accustomed to seeing it from up there." She pointed a finger upward.

"That's my preference." He gazed into the distance. "You're right about the perspective. When I look at the charts I find myself recalling what it looks like from the air. It helps with navigating down here where everything is one dimensional." He slid up the sunglasses, gave her a quick, appreciative look. "Most people wouldn't think about that."

Darn him! Just when she had him figured out he had to go and say something nice. "Maybe I'm just trying to make myself feel better, knowing that you're so familiar with the area."

"You were nervous? I can assure you, you're in very good hands."

Was that the beginnings of a smile she saw on his lips? She'd never know. He lowered the sunglasses, settling them on the bridge of his nose. He had retreated again.

She left the wheelhouse and headed for the galley. At least there she was in her own element. She knew how things worked—which ingredients to combine to achieve a desired result. That couldn't be said for her dealings with Gray. Abrasive one minute, complimentary the next. He was too unpredictable for words. Or was it that unpredictability that fascinated her? Her steps slowed. There—she had just admitted it. He fascinated her.

"Great lunch, Erin. If that's any indication of what you can do I understand why David stole you away from your former employer." Bill handed his dishes to Angela, who set about washing them.

Erin gave him an odd look. "How do you know about that?"

"David's an old friend of mine." He grinned. "He was mighty pleased that you agreed to come to work for him."

She flushed with pleasure at the compliment. "He can be persuasive."

"I know. He's the one who talked me into recuperating for a while at The Lodge. Speaking of which, I'm going back up on deck." He ascended the steep set of stairs with very little effort, watched carefully by the two women.

"Did you notice the color coming back into his face? I think this trip is going to be good for him." Angela opened cupboard doors until she found the right one, then put the dishes away.

"He told you about his heart operation, I take it." Erin poured herself some coffee.

"Not really. I mean, not voluntarily. But he asked me for some water and I saw the pills he was taking. My Dad had bypass surgery last year, and he took the same ones. I wanted to know, so I asked him." She glanced up the stairwell, as though he might come back. "He's a sweetheart of a man. Now I can watch out for him as well."

Erin smiled at the other woman. "You're something else, you know?"

Angela gave her a saucy grin. "Yeah, I know. Now, do you want any help with dinner or should I clear out of your way?"

"I made a start when I was putting lunch together, so there isn't much left to do."

"In that case I'm going to lie down for a nap. The sea air always makes me tired."

"Have you ever seen anything so beautiful?" Bill was standing at the railing when Erin went back out on deck. As usual, time had sped by while she worked in the kitchen. They had completed the crossing of open water and were now threading their way between the mainland and a string of islands to their left. A small colony of seals was hauled out on a rocky outcrop, barking their displeasure at being disturbed.

"Wow." Erin shaded her eyes. "I see what you mean."

Secluded coves dusted with fine white sand and strewn with driftwood called to the beachcomber in her. The islands acted like a breakwater and the boat moved easily through relatively calm water. "I didn't know it was so . . ." she searched for the right word. "So intimate." On most of the islands, tall trees grew right down to the high water mark, providing a stark dark backdrop for the pale sand of the gently curved coves.

"More people should see this," Bill said, almost to himself. "It's true wilderness." He turned to her. "Did you know that some of the native tribes used to put their young men alone on an island as a coming of age test?"

"I didn't know that. Do they still do it?"

"I don't know." He returned his gaze to the islands. "But I think it was a good idea. I wish we had a custom like that. Teach our young men some self-reliance."

Erin laughed and he gave her an odd look. "What's so funny?"

She shook her head. "I wasn't laughing at what you said. As a matter of fact, I agree that it's a good idea. No, I was thinking about the farewell party my friends at the restaurant gave me. Somebody came up with the idea of giving me things I'd need to survive '*way up there in the north*'."

"Had any of them ever been farther north than Nanaimo?"

"I doubt it. At least not judging by the gifts I got. When you mentioned self-reliance it reminded me. I received a book on edible plants."

"Sounds useful. You could start a whole new trend at The Lodge."

Erin grinned. "It's a possibility, but I rather think the customers prefer a good steak."

"I suspect you're right." He gave her a sideways glance. "Are you nervous about starting the new job?"

"Not a bit." Erin brightened, happy to converse on her favorite subject. "It's not quite as nerve-wracking as starting a new restaurant. Here at least, the menus are already in place. David has given me *carte blanche* to make changes, but I'd like to take my time. I'm really looking forward to it."

"You're very confident."

"About my work, yes. It's what I've always wanted to do." She held out her hands, looking at them critically. "When I was a child I'd climb up on a chair and stand beside my mother while she baked or while she prepared dinner." A wave of nostalgia caught her unaware, and she blinked rapidly, fighting to retain her composure. "She died when I was fourteen. Sometimes I can't remember what she looked like, but I can still see her hands. The veins on the backs of her hands were visible right through the skin. The two things I remember the most are making sugar cookies at Christmas, and watching her peel potatoes."

"And that's why you became a chef?"

She looked at the older man with a sad smile. "It probably had something to do with it."

"Where did you take your training?"

"My formal training was in Vancouver but my real training—you know, the sort of thing they don't tell you about in school, was at a hotel in Victoria. That's where I learned what it's really like to work in a big kitchen." She gave her head a quick, emphatic shake. "Good experience, but not the type of place I'd like to spend my career. Do you know that an executive chef rarely gets a chance to cook? Now that's downright crazy. All that skill, all that talent and he sits in an office most of the day doing paperwork." She waved her hand in the air as though brushing aside a totally unacceptable situation. "I'd never want to get stuck in something like that."

"Can't say I blame you." He gave her an understanding smile. "There's nothing like hands-on."

"Been there, done that, huh?" She looked at him curiously. "Did anyone ever tell you that you're very good at getting people to talk about themselves without giving away anything about yourself?"

"I'm not trying to be secretive, it's just that I enjoy hearing about other people." A shadow flickered across his face, then was gone. "Nothing like bypass surgery to remind one that there's so much more to learn." He turned away from the railing and sat down again. "So what else did you get?"

Erin frowned.

"At your going away party. What else?"

"Oh that." She sat down across from him. "You'll appreciate this. I got a Popiel Pocket Fisherman."

"You're kidding. That's wonderful."

"It's still in its original box and everything. The restaurant hostess found it at a garage sale. The fishing line had deteriorated over time, so she even bought me a new spool of line and a couple of lures."

"Then we won't starve." Bill checked his watch. "It

must be the fresh air, but I'm hungry again. I talked to Gray while you were below, and we should be stopping any time. He plans to go only as far as Ben usually goes the first day."

"In that case I'll go and make some biscuits. Simple fare tonight. Stew and biscuits."

"Do you think we could eat out here on the deck?" The older man pointed to a bald eagle on a nearby island. It was so close they could see the yellow talons gripping the branch of a dead tree. "I hate to miss a minute of this."

"I don't see why not." As she spoke the pitch of the engines changed and the boat slowed. "I'll serve it up in some large soup bowls I found in the galley." She touched him lightly on the shoulder. "Still want that second cup of coffee?"

"After dinner if that's all right with you."

"Perfect." She headed toward the narrow doorway leading below. "See you in a little while."

Chapter Three

"You weren't kidding about fattening me up." Angela patted her flat stomach. "I'm glad we're only on this boat for a few days 'cause I surely can't resist your cooking."

Erin flushed at the compliment. "I'm glad you enjoyed it." She gathered up the bowls, smiling to herself as she noticed that the men had cleaned up every scrap of their second helpings. The biscuits had completely disappeared—including the extras she'd made to have as a snack later on.

Angela followed her to the galley a moment later. "I was just checking to see if Bill wanted me to bring up his evening medication, but he has it with him." She filled the sink with water and started on the dishes. "You take the coffee up and I'll join you in a minute."

* * *

Bill and Gray had their heads together when Erin went back onto the deck, their voices carrying easily in the cool evening air. Gray had anchored the boat on the lee side of an island. Slanting through the trees, the sun's rays angled into the water and disappeared in the depths below the boat.

". . . made better time than I thought today." Gray accepted the mug of coffee with a nod.

Bill rumbled his appreciation then continued the conversation. "The boat sounds as though it has a hefty power plant. What's it got?"

"Twin one thirty-five's. They're almost new, and Ben is a stickler for service. He had a short in the electrical system the week before last and he insisted that they give it a complete going over." Gray shrugged. "Can't say I blame him, though. His contract with The Lodge calls for delivery of diesel and gasoline every week and he wants to keep it. The fuel goes down below in the hatch and the stuff up here on the deck is gravy." He looked at Erin directly for the first time since she'd come back up on deck. "Speaking of gravy, that was probably the best stew I've ever tasted."

"Only probably?" Erin grinned. Was she really teasing him?

"Okay, Okay. It was definitly the best I've ever tasted." He took a swallow of coffee. "And now if you've finished fishing for compliments, the surgery is open."

"Surgery? What's going on?" Bill looked from one to the other.

Dark blue eyes met Erin's and her heart skipped a beat.

"Erin got a sliver in her hand this morning." He fished in the pocket of his jeans and pulled out a jackknife. "This is super sharp. I don't think it'll hurt much, but if you like, you can numb the area with an ice cube first."

"My hands are pretty tough. I'll be fine." She hoped she wouldn't disgrace herself.

"Shouldn't we at least have some ointment and a Band-Aid on hand?" Bill stood up. "Where is the first aid kit?"

"Down below on the kitchen side of the forward bulkhead."

"Right. I knew I'd seen it somewhere." The older man scurried off.

"I think he has a queasy stomach." He held out his hand, wiggling his fingers. "Here, let me have another look before we lose our light."

She offered her hand palm-up. He accepted it gently and without further warning brought it to his lips. Liquid fire sizzled through her veins and she pulled back. "What are you doing?" she gasped, startled.

"Try it for yourself." He lifted her hand toward her face. "It's inflamed. You can feel the heat with your lips."

"Oh." She lowered her head, trying to hide her disappointment. How could she have been so foolish as to think he was kissing her hand? "I knew that."

He opened the knife and the blade glinted in the last of the sunlight. "Let's do it then."

Taking a deep breath she spread her fingers wide, stretching the skin tightly across her palm. She wished she'd opted for the ice cube, but it was too late to chicken out.

"Hold still now."

A sharp prick followed his words and she tensed, waiting for the pain.

"Got it." He held the sliver in front of her eyes. "That sucker was ready to come out."

"All finished?" Bill came out onto the deck with an armful of supplies.

"And the patient is still alive." Gray briskly poured a capful of peroxide over the raw flesh. "That's good," he said to himself as it bubbled and foamed. He patted it dry, applied ointment and a large Band-Aid then looked up at her with a wry grin. "You deserve a lollipop for being such a good girl, but I'm fresh out."

"Aw shucks." Erin studied her hand. "You did that well. I took a St. John's ambulance course this spring and I couldn't have done it better myself."

"Why did you do that?" He shot her a curious look. "Any particular reason?"

"I don't know." She started to gather up the first aid supplies then turned back to find him watching her carefully. "No, that's not true. I do know. I'd read a book about a family that had been stranded out in the middle of nowhere when their light plane went down and the story stayed with me for days. What if something like that happened to me? Could I make it? So I started reading about survival, and when the St John's course was offered at Camosun College I signed up." She was suddenly self-conscious. "Sorry. Didn't mean to make such a speech."

"No. It's interesting." Gray was studying her over the rim of his mug.

"Is that why one of your friends gave you the book

on edible plants?" asked Bill. He turned to Gray. "Her friends threw her a farewell party, with gifts that could help her survive '*way up there in the North*'."

Erin flushed, unaccustomed to being the center of attention. "The book was more of a joke than anything, I think."

Gray set down the mug and leaned forward, elbows on his knees. "It might have been meant that way, but a person could survive out there by knowing what plants to eat." He looked toward the mainland where dense stands of trees marched into the distance.

Erin followed the direction of his gaze, surprised to see that the treetops were no longer tipped with gold. The sun had slid into the sea as they were speaking, leaving only a blush of color on the clouds that hung over the western horizon.

She headed for the stairwell, clutching the First Aid supplies. "Let's hope none of us ever has to find out what that's like."

"What what's like?" Angela ran lightly up the stairs, looking from Erin to the men for an explanation.

"We were talking about surviving out there." Bill inclined his head toward the mainland.

Erin gave him a grateful glance and started down the stairs.

"I've been meaning to ask you something." Angela directed her question at Gray. "Why are we towing a boat? It looks similar to my husband's zodiac but not quite as sturdy."

Halfway down the stairs Erin paused. She'd been wondering the same thing.

Gray stood up and walked to the stern. "It was given to Ben just the other day. It's mainly for emergencies, but he thought it might be fun to go on shore when he anchors for the night. As soon as he gets a few dollars ahead he's going to install davits so he won't have to tow it, but in the meantime, it's fine where it is."

"Oh. Okay." Angela's voice drifted down the stairs. "I really came up here to say goodnight. I had a nap this afternoon but I'm still tuckered out."

"I won't be far behind you," Bill said to the retreating figure. Stifling a yawn, he stood up and joined Gray at the stern. "What's the weather forecast for tomorrow?"

"Rainy during the early part of the day, but there are slickers in that storage locker where the chairs were stored, if you want to spend some time on deck."

"Good, good." Bill clapped a hand on the younger man's shoulder. "Goodnight then. What time do you plan to get underway?"

"As soon as we've finished breakfast. I'll check with Erin on that, see if she minds whipping up something. Around eight, I'd guess. That will put us well beyond any sign of civilization by the early afternoon."

Bill reached the stairwell as Erin emerged. He stood aside, gripping the handrail.

"Are you all right?" She checked his eyes. "You look tired," she said quietly.

"A bit," he admitted. "But it's been a wonderful day. See you both in the morning." He headed below and Erin watched him carefully.

"Looks like you've taken a liking to him." Gray

sauntered across the deck and folded himself into one of the chairs.

"What's not to like?" She smiled to soften the words.

"You've got that right." He took off his cap and ran his fingers through short, curly hair. The gray hair she'd noticed earlier was evenly scattered over his head. He suddenly seemed human.

"Listen," she said hesitantly. "I heard you talking to Bill earlier. "I don't mind doing the breakfast at all."

He raised his head. "Eavesdropping, were you?"

She lifted her shoulders and spread her hands, a gesture learned from many French co-workers. "You weren't exactly whispering."

"Fair enough." In spite of the gathering darkness, his eyes glittered with amusement. "I didn't want to ask you 'cause it doesn't seem fair. Tell you what—I'll talk to Ben about refunding your fare. That's the least he can do."

"Please don't do that." She frowned, searching for the right words to convince him. "I'm enjoying it, and besides, I can afford the fare. I got a generous signing bonus from The Lodge."

In the space of a few seconds, his body tensed and the smile disappeared. "Of course. David Kendall knows how to get what he wants."

Erin's first instinct was to challenge him, but she managed to hold her tongue. She took a few steps away, pretending to study something in the water then and looking up at the dazzling array of stars. After a few deep, calming breaths she turned back to him. "Why do you dislike David Kendall so much?" she asked softly. "What do you have against him?"

He stared down at the deck, seemingly unable to meet her eyes. "It's a long story," he said finally. Rising from the chair, he moved to the railing, his gait stiff.

He seemed to favor his left leg and she watched him with a critical eye, all thoughts of David Kendall gone from her head. "Are you all right?" She walked to his side, touched his arm. "Have you hurt yourself?" He looked down at her hand and she withdrew it.

"It's okay." He shifted his weight. "Only acts up when I'm tired." He glanced toward the wheelhouse. "Tomorrow I'll take advantage of the captain's stool rather than stand all day."

"Don't tell me you have arthritis. You're far too young." She gave him what she hoped was an encouraging smile.

"Nope." He stood facing the island that lay between them and the open ocean. It was little more than a dark spot against the horizon. He turned toward her, his face pale in the light from the cabin. "You're very persistent, aren't you?"

She nodded.

"I took some shrapnel in Afghanistan. I was there with our peacekeeping forces. Even so, I'm glad I had the experience. We're doing so much good over there."

"How did it happen?" She was surprised at how badly she wanted to know.

"I was flying helicopters."

"And you got shot down?" Her heart was in her throat.

"Nothing that glamorous, I'm afraid. I was flying

MedEvac, and I'd gone into a village to help bring out a couple of our guys. Someone fired an RPG at us and I took at hit in my left leg." He reached down to massage his thigh. "The doctors tell me they got it out, but it still bothers me when it's cold and wet, or when I'm tired. It also cramps my style on the dance floor."

"Don't joke like that. You could have been killed."

"Yeah." Erin sensed him drawing away from her. "Too many of our guys were."

She forced herself to remain still, waiting for his thoughts to come back to the present. Water lapped against the side of the boat, a rhythmic accompaniment to the comfortable silence.

"Sorry," he said eventually. "I usually don't talk about that stuff."

"So you fly helicopters too," she said, casting about in her mind for some way to change the subject. "Do you like them?"

"Not particularly. I prefer fixed wing aircraft."

"Fixed wing." She took a moment to consider his words. "As opposed to those . . ." she twirled her finger in the air. "On a helicopter."

"The rotors."

"I knew that." She laughed. "So tell me, what type of *fixed wing* airplane do you own for your charter business?"

"Aircraft." He was trying to sound stern, but a faint smile gave him away. "Might as well learn the correct terminology. I have a Mallard."

"Like the duck?"

"Yeah." Even in the faint light from the cabin she

could see his features softening. "She's a beauty. Made by Grumman. They also made the Widgeon and the Goose, but for my money, the Mallard's their finest aircraft." For a moment she thought she saw a challenge in his eyes. "I'll take you up for a ride one day after you're settled."

"Really? I'd love that!" She didn't care if she sounded eager, because she was.

He chuckled softly, a low, intimate sound that sent a shimmer of desire dancing across her skin. "It's a deal then. But first things first. We've got a long day tomorrow. I'd better get some sleep."

She nodded her agreement. "Me too." She took a few steps toward the stairwell then turned to find him watching her. "I'll have breakfast ready by seven," she said, wondering what was going through his head. "See you in the morning."

"Goodnight Erin." He turned away to stare into the night. She went downstairs, removed her clothes and fell asleep moments after her head hit the pillow.

Gray stared into the inky water. His conversation with Erin had triggered an avalanche of memories. The mental images of his time served in Afghanistan haunted him relentlessly, and there were times when he was convinced that they would never fade. The ruthlessness of the warlords, the eagerness of the young children to attend school, the stark beauty of the countryside. These images were interwoven with the tight, gut-wrenching fear that had gripped him every time he flew a mission, knowing that there were wounded men clinging to life, awaiting his arrival. Knowing that remnants of the Taliban grew stronger every day, that every one of them hunted the Allied troops with high-powered rifles, RPGs and shoulder-fired missiles.

A bank of fog rolled out of the darkness. He looked up into the sky, but the stars had disappeared. Fine mist fell on his face, and as though on cue his leg started to throb again. Served him right, he though angrily. What had he been thinking, confiding in Erin, talking about his wound? He had come dangerously close to lowering the barriers he'd so carefully erected. And that comment about dancing! He'd almost blurted out the story that up until now he'd shared only with Ben. How, when his girlfriend Holly had seen his scar, she'd averted her eyes, but not before he glimpsed her repugnance.

He should have been prepared for her reaction. After all, he'd always known that Holly was obsessed with appearances. She loved to be seen on his arm, fair and petite in contrast to his tall, dark good looks. Most of all, she loved to dance. He absently rubbed his thigh, thoughts drifting into dangerous territory. He knew instinctively that if Erin had been his girlfriend she wouldn't have minded that a little shrapnel had slowed him down. He also knew that if he'd been foolish enough to feel sorry for himself she would have pulled him up short.

He felt his lips curve in a reluctant smile. She was a handful, all right. Feisty, smart, and not afraid to take him on. And she was the first woman he'd looked at twice since Holly.

"Forget it pal," he said aloud as he made one last

round of the deck, checking to ensure that the boat was firmly anchored. "Just forget it."

"Now that," said Gray, pushing his empty plate away, "was delicious." He smiled at Erin as she set a plate in front of Bill. "Thanks."

"You're welcome." She topped up his coffee mug and whisked his plate away, aware of his eyes on her. He was different this morning. For that matter, so was she. Their conversation last night had lasted only a few minutes, but it had changed the dynamic between them. No longer antagonists, they were now on the same side, and it felt good. Humming softly to herself, she tidied up the galley.

"Sorry I'm late." Angela slid back the partition to the forward sleeping quarters. Sensibly attired this morning, she wore a dark blue fleece outfit with a T-shirt and sneakers. Even so, she managed to look fresh and put together.

Erin looked down at her own jeans and wondered if it was too late to develop a sense of style. Her oldest running shoes peeked out beyond the bell-bottoms of the jeans. Solid and comfortable, they were the shoes she used on long rambling walks along China Beach, outside of Victoria. A hooded sweatshirt completed her outfit.

"How's the weather out there?" Angela inquired, peering up the stairwell at the grey sky. She poured herself a mug of coffee and slid onto the bench across from Bill.

"Drizzly," replied Gray. "Just about what they forecast yesterday." He stood up and placed his mug in the small sink. "I'd best get started."

"Good coffee, Erin." Bill drank slowly, savoring every sip.

Erin sat down beside him, mug in hand. It was odd, but she hadn't felt hungry this morning.

"Aren't you going to eat?" he asked. "Or did you already have something."

"Maybe later." She looked across at Angela. "I put yours in the oven to keep warm. I hope you don't mind, but it was easier to make it all at once."

"Don't be silly." Angela stirred a miniscule amount of sugar into her coffee. "Oh, what the heck," she said with a grin, adding a generous teaspoon. "Life's too short."

"Amen to that." Bill saluted her with his cup. "Well ladies, time's a-wasting." Erin slid out of the booth and he got to his feet. "Even if it is raining, I'm going to go outside and enjoy myself." He picked up a pair of binoculars from the bench. "I'm prepared in case some orcas swim by." He shrugged into a jacket and climbed the stairs.

Erin watched him go. "What a nice man," she said, turning to Angela.

"You know, I've been trying to remember where I know him from, but it's just not there." Angela tapped her temple. "When he talked about recognizing me, I had the oddest feeling that I should know who he is, too."

"Maybe it will come to you." Erin retrieved the plate from the oven and set it in front of the other woman. Perfectly browned sausages accompanied thick slices of French toast.

"Now I know you were serious about fattening me up." Angela narrowed her eyes as she poured syrup over the French toast. "I'll bet you didn't serve this to Bill, did you?"

Erin sat back down to watch her friend eat, then drew back in surprise. When had she started thinking of Angela as a friend? "Much to his disgust, I gave him tomato slices and toast. Oh, and two sausages. They're low-fat chicken sausages."

Angela took a small bite. "Pretty good." She dug in enthusiastically, looking up when the rattle of the anchor chain echoed through the cabin.

"What in the world was that?" Erin asked, startled at the unfamiliar sound.

"Sounds like we're getting underway." Seconds after Angela spoke the powerful motors rumbled to life. "I think I'll go up and sit with Bill—even if it *is* raining." Angela popped the last piece of French toast into her mouth and took her plate to the sink. "What are you going to do?" she asked, washing and drying her dishes with brisk, efficient movements.

"The same, I think." Reaching into the wardrobe by the forward sleeping compartment, she caught sight of herself in the full-length mirror attached to the back of the door. With a sigh, she closed the door and turned to see Angela watching her.

"I know what you see when you look in the mirror. You see the same thing every woman sees." She gave her head a quick shake. "Why is it that we see faults in ourselves that others never notice?"

Erin waited for several heartbeats, but the anger didn't come. In its place was acceptance of what Angela said.

"Know what we do with the young girls?" Angela walked across the small space and opened the door again. "After we work on their self-esteem issues we concentrate on their assets." She turned Erin to face the mirror. "I'll bet you rarely acknowledge all your good points. Your hair is terrific, you have beautiful skin and your eyes are to die for."

Erin studied her reflection for a moment then leaned closer to the mirror. "Do you really think so?" She turned her head to the left, then to the right. "My eyebrows could use some work though, couldn't they?" She wiggled them up and down, looking at her friend in the mirror.

"Don't touch them," commanded Angela, "and I tell you what. On your first break from The Lodge, call me in Victoria and I'll take you to see my aesthetician. She's famous for her brow jobs."

"You're kidding!" Erin couldn't believe her ears. "You mean someone is actually known for doing people's eyebrows?"

"But of course!" Angela gave Erin's shoulders an affectionate squeeze. "You haven't lived until you've had your brows shaped."

"If you say so." Erin rolled her eyes, then took one last look in the mirror. "I'm beginning to think there might be hope for me yet."

Angela pumped her fist. "You know it, girl!"

Swathed in a dark green slicker, Bill sat in a chair, feet propped up on the lower rail. Erin and Angela donned slickers as well, and pulled up chairs on either side of him. The drizzle had stopped, and a weak sun was trying to break through the high overcast.

"Wow, look at that." Erin studied the shore of the mainland as the boat cut through the surprisingly calm water. Thick mist hung in vertical strands between the tall trees. "It looks as though the trees are smouldering."

"It does, doesn't it?" Bill nodded slowly. "It takes some getting used to. The first few times I traveled up the coast by boat I kept thinking that there must be homes tucked in the trees, and that I was seeing smoke from the chimneys."

"It's not like that all the time, is it?" Erin tried to picture the landscape in the sun. Bleached logs littered the high water mark of the shoreline, and beyond that the trees seemed to stretch into infinity.

"No. The sun can burn it off in a matter of minutes." Bill picked up his binoculars to follow the flight of a bald eagle. "But they don't call it the rain forest for nothing."

"I suppose not." Erin copied Bill's position, propping her feet on the low railing. "Peaceful though, isn't it?"

"That it is." He tucked his binoculars inside the rain slicker and gave an audible sigh. "I haven't felt this relaxed for years." He smiled at Angela then lapsed into silence. The drone of the motors faded into the background as the trio sat quietly, lost in their own thoughts.

Moments later the solitude was broken by a gust of air. A fine geyser of water sparkled in the feeble sunlight, followed by a sleek black body, topped by the unmistakable black fin. The orca surfaced not more than fifty feet from the boat, blowhole opening wide as it took in air.

Bill's feet thumped on the deck as he stood up, gripping the railing with one hand and fumbling for his binoculars with the other. "It's a pod of orcas," he gasped as several more fins broke the surface. "Aren't they the most beautiful things you've ever seen?" He held the binoculars in his right hand, not attempting to use them. The orcas were close enough that the cheek markings were clearly visible.

"They're travelling," he said as the pod swam parallel to the boat, breaking the surface at regular intervals. "Probably looking for a school of fish."

Erin looked up into the wheelhouse. Gray nodded to her, a broad smile transforming his face. Her heart beat a little faster and she wondered if she was imagining something that wasn't there. She gave him a tentative smile and turned back just as the orcas slipped into high gear, surging ahead of the boat and crossing in front of the bow.

Bill raised his binoculars. "They're heading into the open ocean," he said, watching until they were swallowed up in a bank of fog. "I counted eleven." He turned to Angela. "Did you count?"

"It's hard with them going up and down all the time but I counted ten. Could have been eleven." She looked at Erin. "How many did you get?"

Erin pulled a face. "I didn't know I was supposed to count. I was just enjoying the spectacle."

"Ignore me. I'm glad you got to see them." Bill frowned. "It's just that I'm concerned about their future. There's a pod to the south of us in Puget Sound that's in trouble, and even up here, where there's less pollution, the numbers are dwindling dramatically." His face brightened. "But those ones looked healthy. That's a good sign." Another eagle flew by. "And there are lots of eagles, which means there are plenty of fish. Things are looking up." Easing himself back into the deck chair he resumed his former position.

"I'm going to go down below and get my binoculars too." Erin paused. "Anybody want anything?"

Bill shook his head. "No thanks," said Angela. "We're fine."

Erin pulled her duffel bag out from under the cot and tossed it on the mattress. The lights flickered and she looked up, annoyed. It was going to be hard enough to find the binoculars as it was. She didn't need any grief from the electrical system. "Now where did I put them?" she asked herself, thinking back to the morning she'd done her final packing. Had that only been two days ago? She fought with the ties of her duffel bag, trying to undo the knots. Perhaps it had only been two days, but it felt like a lifetime ago. She dropped the ties and opened the door of the wardrobe, checking her reflection in the mirror. The woman who looked back had changed in that short time. Perhaps not in appearance, but inside, where it counted. There was a new determination in her eyes. She stepped closer to the mirror. Okay, perhaps not steely determination, the way it would be described in a novel, but there was strength there that had been missing before.

As she stood looking at herself, she recognized a truth that had been staring her in the face for years. How had she missed it? She excelled at her profession.

That much was clear. But when her long workday was over, and she'd poured all her energy into running a busy kitchen, she had nothing left—no energy to stand up to her sister. As Crystal had wheedled and demanded, she'd found it easier to give in. And in doing so, she'd lost respect for herself.

The lights flickered again and went out. Light from the stairwell lit the cabin, and her reflection was nothing more than an outline. "I'll never be that person again," she said firmly, closing the door. "From now on, I'm going to do what's good for me."

The lights winked off and on again. Erin grabbed her duffel bag and shoved it in front of her, up the stairwell. At least on the deck there was plenty of light.

Chapter Four

Erin came back onto the deck and Gray smiled to himself. While she'd been below his eyes kept returning to her empty chair. Now that she was back, a warm sensation bloomed in his chest and he stepped forward, watching her with interest. What was she doing with her duffel bag? She hauled it over beside her chair and sat down, slicker billowing out around her. She said something to Bill and Angela and they all laughed. He would love a cup of coffee, but he hesitated to ask her to make it. As though feeling his eyes on her she looked up and tapped her watch, pantomiming raising a cup to her lips. Nodding, he clutched at his throat and she laughed and disappeared below.

Settling onto the comfortable stool he returned his attention to running the boat. They'd come out from behind a long, narrow island and were getting into heavier seas. He remembered this stretch of desolate coastline from his many flights. A string of smaller islands to the starboard sat between their position and the mainland, but he opted to stay out here in deeper water, where navigation was easier. He automatically checked the depth finder. The display dimmed, and for a moment he wondered if he'd imagined it. He looked again, and at that moment the screen went black. Tapping it impatiently, his eyes flew to the rest of his instruments. None of them were on. He pushed the throttle forward, and the motors dug in, lifting the bow by a few degrees. Bill turned in his chair and looked up at the wheelhouse, a frown creasing his brow. Gray eased the throttle back, trying to recall the older man's words last night. They'd been discussing the electrical short, and how Ben had insisted on a complete check of the electrical service. Bill's words had been eerily prophetic. "It's been my experience," he'd said with a wry grin, "that something always goes wrong right after a major overhaul."

"Looks like he was right," he said to himself, as the boat crested a long, lazy swell then slid down into the trough beyond it. Bill looked up again, and Gray beckoned to him.

The older man walked unsteadily to the wheelhouse, holding the railing as he stepped up. "What is it?"

Gray pointed to the dark screens. "I've lost power to the electronics. Could you steer for a couple of minutes while I go down below and check things out?" He did his best to sound unconcerned, but he could tell the other man wasn't fooled.

"Listen, son." Bill laid a hand on his shoulder. "What's the worst thing that can happen? We anchor in a sheltered spot and call for help?" He paused, waiting for a response. When he got none, he tightened his grip. "Right?"

Gray nodded reluctantly.

"Okay then. Off you go." Bill took hold of the wheel. "You'll figure it out."

Gray grabbed the railings and slid down the stairwell, feet barely touching the steps.

Erin looked up, her face clouded. "Gray, there's something wrong here." The lights flickered. "The coffeemaker won't work, and the lights are acting up again."

His head came up. "Again?"

"Yeah. I came down to dig out my binoculars earlier, and they were flickering on and off. I finally gave up and took my duffel bag out onto the deck."

Prickles of apprehension crawled up his neck at her words. "I wish you'd told me," he said, trying to keep his voice steady, "but never mind that now." Disappearing into the aft sleeping area he headed for the narrow door between the two bunks. The electrical panel was located in the engine room, on the bulkhead wall to the right. He tugged on the door handle then pulled his hand back with a gasp of pain, staring at it in disbelief. He turned to Erin. "Fire extinguisher," he said, pointing to the small red canister mounted on the wall.

She tore it free and handed it to him. "Shall I run up and get the other one from upstairs?"

"Good idea," he said, glad to give her something to do. His mind raced. Beyond the engine room, in the former fish hold, forty-five-gallon drums of gasoline and diesel fuel awaited delivery to The Lodge. A wave of fear stabbed at him, turning his legs to jelly as he watched Erin run up the stairs. "But I have a feeling it's too late," he said to himself.

Using his jacket as a makeshift glove, he opened the door, stepping back as smoke billowed out, followed by the sharp, acrid smell of an electrical fire. Clutching the fire extinguisher, he threw up his arms to protect his face, and the hair on his arms sizzled and burned off.

"Think," he told himself, retreating from the heat. His first instinct was to run to the wheelhouse and issue a Mayday, but with a sinking sensation in the pit of his stomach he recalled Ben showing him the new electrical panel. The radio was on the same circuit as the electronics; calling for help was not an option. There was only one thing to do. He had to go back into the engine room to find out how far the fire had spread—and he had to do it now! He grabbed a damp tea towel from the rack beside the sink, threw it over his head and cracked the seal on the fire extinguisher. Taking a deep breath, he forced himself to move forward, moving the bulky red canister in a steady stream from left to right, then concentrating on the right hand corner of the room, where the electrical panel was situated. He depressed the lever until the extinguisher was empty, then threw it down with a groan of frustration. The heat was becoming unbearable and common sense told him that a fire this intense must already have taken a firm hold. For a moment the fumes from the extinguisher blocked his vision, but when the air started to clear he could see farther into the engine room. He gasped in horror. The fire had climbed the wall and was racing across the ceiling, hot tongues of flame licking at the wood, devouring everything in its path. At this rate it would burn through into the hold in a matter of minutes.

He backed out of the room, shut the door and turned, running into Erin. The extinguisher in her hands looked like a toy compared with what would be needed to subdue this fire. His thoughts raced. If he went up on deck and opened the hatch he could drop down and use the extinguisher on the other side of the wall. But that was like trying to shoot a grizzly with a pea-shooter. Besides, the fresh air would feed the flames the moment they broke through the wall.

He took the canister from Erin, set it on the counter and grabbed her by the arms. Her eyes darted to the door of the engine room, but she stayed calm, and he gave a quick, silent prayer of thanks for her presence. He took a deep breath. "I need your help," he said, hoping that he was conveying confidence. "I need you go get everybody in the boat."

"The boat?" She looked at him, puzzled, then comprehension dawned. "Oh, you mean that inflatable we're towing? Why?"

"Because the fire is going to break through the wall any minute now. And we're carrying a cargo of gasoline and diesel."

She drew herself up. "It's serious, isn't it," she stated calmly.

"Fraid so." He dropped his arms and stood back. "I'll go up with you and make sure you get loaded safely."

"You're coming, aren't you?" For the first time she

looked frightened. "You're not going to do anything heroic, are you?"

"Of course not. But I owe it to Ben to do everything I can to put out the fire."

She gave him a look that melted his heart. "Dammit Gray, don't you go getting yourself killed. I was just starting to like you."

Her words game him the strength he needed. "Glad to hear it. Now let's go."

Erin scrambled up the stairs ahead of Gray.

"What are you two doing . . ." Angela's words faded as she saw Erin's face. "Erin?" she said, reaching out to her friend. "What's going on? Why is Bill steering the boat?"

"There's a fire in the engine room." Erin had no time for niceties. "Gray wants us in the inflatable, just in case."

"But . . ." Angela's eyes darted to the wheelhouse, where Gray having a heated conversation with Bill. "Are you sure?"

"Please Angela. Let's do as he asks. He has enough to think about without a couple of mutinous women on his hands."

"I suppose." She hesitated for a moment, then followed Erin to the stern.

"What do we do?" Erin looked at the little inflatable trailing behind them. "We have to haul it closer, I guess."

"Here, I'll do that." Gray and Bill appeared beside them and Erin became aware that the boat had stopped its forward motion. Gray reached over the rail and a section opened, swinging aside like a gate. "I want the three of you in here as quickly as possible." Hand over hand he pulled on the rope, then held the inflatable alongside the grid.

Angela was first to get in then Gray assisted Bill, who sat down quickly, centering himself on the wooden seat. Erin looked back to see smoke wafting out from the stairwell and was about to get in when she spotted her duffel bag and ran across the deck to pick it up. Gray saw her intention and hesitated, then motioned her into the inflatable. She tossed her bag ahead of her then climbed down, settling onto the wooden seat beside Angela. Gray released the inflatable then climbed back onto the deck. They floated free, still tethered to the boat.

"I don't like this," Erin muttered unhappily. "Couldn't you talk him out of it?" She addressed her remarks to Bill. "There's no way he can put out that fire."

"I think he knows that, but he wants to try." The older man fumbled under his rain slicker and drew out a container of pills, shaking one out into his hand. Tossing it into his mouth, he swallowed then continued talking. "He's always taken chances, ever since he was a young boy."

"You sound like you know him well." Erin talked to cover her nervousness, tensing as Gray disappeared down the stairwell.

"I should. I'm his godfather."

"Really?" She wanted to ask more, but her attention was focused on the spot where Gray had disappeared. Minutes seemed to stretch into hours while smoke poured out and was whipped away on the stiff breeze that had come up suddenly. Just as she was about to panic, Gray stumbled out, falling onto the deck on his hands and knees, sucking in fresh air.

"Gray!" Erin tried to stand up but Angela pulled her back down. She felt helpless, bobbing around in the small boat at the end of a twenty-foot rope.

Gray staggered across the deck and paused, failure clearly written on his face. Bill picked up a paddle and tried to maneuver closer to the boat, his movements clumsy and ineffectual in the bulky rain slicker. Gray got to his feet, ran to the stern and started hauling in the rope. He looked different, and Erin realized that his eyebrows and eyelashes had been scorched away. His fingers fumbled with the knot that secured the rope to the back of the boat. Swollen with seawater, it wouldn't budge and he muttered under his breath, trying to keep his balance as the boat rose and fell on the rising seas.

"Cut the damn thing!" shouted Bill. "Use your jack-knife."

Gray looked up, and for a fleeting moment his eyes were unfocused. Then he gave a brief nod, reached into his pocket and pulled out a jackknife. The rope parted cleanly and he snapped the knife closed and stuck it in his back pocket. With the rope in his hand, he was about to step into the inflatable when the stern of the boat rose precipitously. The sudden movement slammed him sideways into the railing, his free hand scrabbling for a hold. Face contorted with pain he steadied himself, and timing the next swell he stepped into the inflatable, falling in a heap at Bill's feet.

"Row," he croaked, his voice hoarse. "Get us away from her." Stretching out on the bottom of the boat he cradled his shoulder, his face white.

"Angela and I should row," said Erin firmly. "The oarlocks are here beside this seat, and Bill isn't strong enough yet." She turned and offered the older man a weak smile. "Sorry, but it's true."

"No, no. You're right, but take off the slickers. They just get in the way." He slid the oar forward and Erin shrugged out of the slicker then fitted the oar into the holder while Angela did the same on her side of the bench. After a few clumsy attempts they began to pull in unison, increasing the distance between themselves and the boat with every stroke.

For several moments the only sounds were the labored breathing of the two women, and the splash of the oars in the water. Smoke continued to pour out from the boat and was snatched away more quickly than before by the increasing breeze.

"Even the wind is against us," muttered Gray, his gaze not wavering from the boat. "A column of smoke would be a beacon to another ship in the area but this way . . ." he shook his head.

The women stopped rowing, oars trailing in the water as they watched the boat. "What's going to happen now?" Angela gave voice to everyone's thoughts. "Is there any chance that anything will be left?" Her voice was high—childlike almost, and Erin grabbed her hand, willing her silently to stay calm.

"Well." Gray tore his gaze away from the boat and looked at each of them. He was still slumped in the bow of the inflatable but had regained a bit of color. "Diesel fuel ignites very slowly, but gasoline . . ." further words were drowned out by a massive explosion and his head snapped back toward the boat. Four sets of eyes watched in horror as the hatch cover flew into the air, surrounded by fragments of the deck. A ball of flame erupted from the bowels of the boat, brilliant orange outlined with black. They watched, dismayed and fascinated at the same time as another explosion blew the wheelhouse apart. The water around the boat seemed to rise several inches, the surface quivering and bubbling like a cauldron of witches' brew. Then, without fanfare, the boat sank by the stern and slipped below the waves. Nothing remained on the surface but a few pieces of splintered wood and escaping bubbles from the small pockets of air trapped in the rapidly sinking boat.

Gray continued to stare at the spot where the boat had disappeared, shaking his head from side to side. "There should have been something more I could do, but I can't for the life of me think what that would be." He turned to Bill, his eyes bleak. "I don't know how I'm going to tell Ben."

"It won't be easy," said Bill with a crooked grin. "But first things first. Where are we?"

Gray tried to stand up but fell back again. "My shoulder," he said through gritted teeth. "I think I've dislocated it." Using his good arm, he pushed himself into a sitting position and looked around. "The mainland is just behind those islands." He pointed to a series of small islands behind them. "And if I recall correctly, there's nothing around here for miles."

"Miles?" said Angela, her eyes widening. "How many miles?"

"Offhand I'd say that we're around a hundred miles from any settlement."

Angela stared at him. "A hundred miles? What about to the south?"

"That *is* the south. To the north—I don't know—it's just a guess, but around a hundred fifty."

"What are we going to do?" Angela's voice rose, then she visibly gained control of her emotions. "I'm sorry, but I'm scared."

Erin exchanged a quick glance with Gray. "You have every right to be afraid," she said calmly. The inflatable rolled in a sickening motion and a wave broke against the side, spraying them with cold, salty water. "But we'd better get rowing. We can't float around out here all day." She met Gray's eyes. "I think we should head for the mainland. There isn't likely to be any fresh water on those islands."

"Good thinking." Twisting around on his seat, Bill answered for Gray. "We have a following breeze, which is good, but it's kicking up some whitecaps."

"Then we'd better get started." Erin gave Angela's shoulders a squeeze. "Come on, kiddo. We need you."

Angela looked startled, but she picked up the oar and steadied herself. "In that case, let's go."

They closed slowly on the islands, their course taking them between the two largest in the center of the chain. Jagged rocks rimmed the shore, and trees crowded down to the waterline, some leaning far out while others lay lifeless in the water, pushed outward by the vigorous growth of the trees behind them.

Bill studied the flow of water between the islands. "Tide's coming in," he remarked as a surge of water picked them up, speeding their passage between the rocks on either side. "Look out," he shouted hoarsely, pointing to a downed tree in the water ahead. Erin craned her neck but the warning came too late. The submerged branches of the tree clawed at the submersible like sharp fangs, tearing a hole in the starboard pontoon just above the water line. The telltale hiss of escaping air galvanized the two women, who pulled with all their strength on the oars.

"Gray," hissed Bill. "Open that locker and see if there's a kit or anything we could use to patch this hole." He pressed a hand against the hole, but succeeded only in making the sound more noticeable.

"No, nothing." Gray turned back. "Just a couple of coffee cans. For baling, I guess."

"Hand one over here." Bill motioned impatiently. "We're going to need them soon, and I'd like to think I'm being of some help."

"How far now?" Erin gasped, not daring to turn around. Every pull of the oar was critical at this point. Her survival book had talked about the cold coastal waters. This far north, water temperatures rose very little in the summer months and she knew one thing for sure. They would not survive long in the water. She thought of Bill and his heart condition. Could he survive without his pills?

"Bill," she asked as she moved forward for the next stroke, "do you have any of your pills with you?"

He nodded. "A few." His gaze darted from the shore to the pontoon, which was deflating quickly. Each wave splashed water into the bottom of the inflatable, and it swirled around their feet, growing deeper with every second. Bill and Gray scooped at it with the coffee tins, but it sloshed around unpredictably with every movement of the waves.

Gray paused, reached into his jacket and pulled out a plastic sandwich bag. Several vials of pills showed clearly through the clear material.

"How did you . . ." Bill continued bailing, but his relief was clear.

"I saw your stash this morning so I knew where to look." Gray shoved the bag of pills back inside his jacket and looked at the older man with obvious affection. "Now let's get busy. I have no intention of going for a swim today."

Minutes passed with no conversation, Gray and Bill desperately scooping out water and tossing it over the side. Angela and Erin expended every ounce of energy they possessed, their feet scrabbling for purchase on the watery floor of the inflatable. Erin looked sideways at her friend. Tears were rolling down Angela's cheeks and her hair whipped across her face, several strands sticking in her lipstick. Erin wondered how she had ever doubted the other woman's strength.

Erin chanced a quick look behind. The beach was closer now, a broad sweep of small rocks smoothed by the ceaseless action of the water. Strands of kelp lay along the high water mark, broad dark leaves glistening at one end while at the other, long stems twined together like giant pasta. Past the kelp, white logs of every size dotted a broad sandy beach and over it all the forest loomed, dark and forbidding.

They closed on the shore, and as though to help them along a sizeable wave lifted the inflatable, depositing the bow firmly on the foreshore. Startled by their abrupt arrival, Gray looked around, taking in their surroundings. Bill dropped the coffee can, his face wreathed in smiles. Angela removed her hands from the oars and Erin gasped in sympathy. The palms of the other woman's hands had blistered and many of the blisters had broken, revealing the raw skin beneath.

"You are the most remarkable woman I've ever met." Erin put both arms around Angela's shoulders, hugging her fiercely. The blond smiled weakly, brushing away her tears with the back of her hand.

"What about *your* hands?" Angela grabbed at Erin's hand, frowning when she saw only one blister among the rough red patches. "How come you don't have any blisters?"

Erin looked at her hands. "Between food prep and cooking, these hands take a beating every day. They've grown tough over the years."

Angela gingerly shoved her hands in the pockets of her jacket. "Lucky you."

Erin waited for Bill to help Gray to a standing position, and they climbed over the good pontoon, rocks crunching noisily under their feet. Angela stood up unsteadily then followed, standing at the water's edge.

The muscles in Erin's arms quivered from the effort of rowing, but she managed to lift her duffel bag and dragged it up onto the sand.

The forlorn party looked around dully, still in shock. They had landed on a curved stretch of beach, anchored on either end by rocky headlands jutting into the sea. Waves broke against these black outcrops and Erin knew that winter storms would hurl water against them with tremendous force, sending spray high into the air.

Gray was the first one to move. He staggered to the bleached skeleton of what had once been a giant of a tree, roots reaching ten or twelve feet up into the sky on one end, while the other lay buried in the fine sand. He sat down, clutching his shoulder with his good hand.

Erin went to him, frowning as she noticed his wet jeans. She shouldn't have been surprised; he'd been sitting flat in the bottom of the boat. "You're wet," she said briskly. "I think you should take your jeans off."

"What? Here, in front of all these people?" He managed to smile at her through the pain, and her heart tapped out a quick staccato against her ribs.

"Why not?" she challenged, wondering where the words had come from. Was she actually flirting with him? It was fun, but this was definitely not the right time. Regretfully, she shifted her attention to his shoulder. "I don't want you going into shock, that's all."

"Don't worry about that. I intend to stick around and see how this turns out." He managed a laugh, then glanced past her to where Bill and Angela stood talking. "Is she going to be all right?" he asked, suddenly serious.

"Yeah, I think she is." She glanced over at the other two, who were slowly walking toward them. "She's tougher than she looks. Her hands are badly blistered from rowing, but I have a first aid kit in my duffel bag. She'll be fine."

"Good. I wish I could say the same for myself." He supported his left arm with his right. "I feel useless."

"Nonsense." Erin raised her voice as the others came nearer. "We wouldn't have made it this far if you hadn't hustled us off the boat like you did."

"She's right," said Bill, pulling down the coarse zipper of the rain slicker and shrugging out of it. "So there'll be no more blaming yourself for what happened." He tossed the slicker over the log. "It was an electrical fire, plain and simple. You couldn't have known it was going to happen." He turned back to Gray. "Was he insured? Ben?"

"Are you kidding?" Gray gazed out to sea. "His father used to own an insurance company in Nanaimo. He's covered for everything."

"There, you see!" Bill grinned. "Now let's concentrate on getting ourselves settled." He looked at Gray expectantly. "What should we do first?"

Gray drew himself up. "First of all, we should pull the inflatable up well beyond the high tide mark. It's no use to us as a boat, but we might find some use for it." He slid off the log and walked behind it. The roots were buried in the sand, forming the end of a U-shaped enclosure. Where it emerged from the roots the trunk was easily six feet across. Another large log, also bare of bark lay parallel to the giant. The separation between the two trunks was approximately eight feet, offering an ideal shelter. "I don't think we need to look any further than right here for a place to set up. It's flat and sandy and sheltered on three sides by logs and those roots. With all the driftwood around, we can even rig up some sort of a roof for tonight." He pointed to the slicker. "We also have the inflatable and three slickers." Just then a shaft of sun broke through the cloud cover. "We're going to be fine. Besides, it could be a lot worse. It could be winter."

"Exactly right!" Erin pushed away from the log and headed toward the shore. "Let's think of this as an adventure." Once at the inflatable, she grabbed onto the remnants of the rope, looping it around her arm and pulling with all her strength.

"It's heavier than it looks, isn't it?" Bill materialized beside her and reached for one of the ropes that circled the remaining pontoon.

"No, Bill," Erin cried, waving him away. "Your heart."

The older man straightened. "You let me be the judge of that." He smiled to soften the words. "Erin you have to trust me on this. I know my limitations. Besides, I was only going to lift it while you pull it up onto the sand. After that I think you can manage it on your own."

And he was right. Once out of the water and over the line of kelp the inflatable slid along the sand with a soft hissing sound. Erin pulled it up beside the roots of the tree trunk. "Now," she said firmly. "I'm going to look at Gray's arm."

Chapter Five

"You said it was dislocated," she said, as he took off his jacket. "Are you sure?" He slid his good arm out of the T-shirt and she pulled it over his head and eased it down over the injured shoulder. He tensed with pain, but made no sound. For one insane moment she was tempted to reach out and touch the rough stubble along the line of his jaw. Avoiding his eyes, she turned her attention back to the shoulder.

"I dislocated it twice before. The medic told me that each time it happens there's more of a chance it'll dislocate again." He frowned down at the offending shoulder. "I guess he knew what he was talking about."

"What did he do?" She was quite sure she knew the answer, but she was delaying.

"He put it back in place. Said something about doing it right away, before the muscles around the joint go

79

into spasms." He looked up at her. "I can walk you through it. I watched what he did."

Erin felt the blood drain out of her face, and she grasped the log for support. "I was afraid you'd say that," she said, her voice little more than a whisper.

"You can do it." He reached out with his good arm and steadied her.

"It's going to hurt, isn't it?" She looked into his eyes.

He nodded. "For a second, yes. But it has to be done." A slow smile spread across his face. "And to tell you the truth I'd like to get it over with."

"All right."

Using hands and words, he painted a picture of how the humerus had dislocated and was now sitting in front of the shoulder blade. Using his good arm, they rehearsed the amount of pressure to use, then he positioned her hands. "Are you ready?" he asked and she nodded. "All right, now!"

Erin applied pressure as he instructed and the humerus slipped back into place. "It worked," she cried, momentarily blinded by tears of relief.

Gray swayed for a moment, then dropped his arm, allowing it to hang loosely by his side. Angela and Bill gathered around, wanting to offer comfort, unsure of what to do.

Erin recovered quickly. "You should have a sling. I know that much." She pulled her duffel bag into the shelter of the logs. "There's a piece of fabric in my first aid kit. That's what it's for." She spread Bill's slicker on the sand and started pulling items out of the bag.

"What in the world is all that?" Gray stood over the pile of items, an expression of disbelief on his face.

Erin looked up sheepishly. "I told you I got a lot of silly stuff at that going-away party." She paused in her search and picked up a battered cardboard box, handing it to Bill. "Remember these? Collapsible cups? They were some of the pseudo-survival gifts I was given."

"I do remember these!" Bill opened the box and took out one of the cups. A series of circular rings of diminishing size sat on his hand. The smallest ring had a flat bottom. Grasping the largest ring, he lifted it up, and the rings snapped into place, forming a cone-shaped cup. "When I was a kid we had a plastic set of these that we'd take on picnics." He grinned delightedly. "I've never seen any in metal before, but it makes sense." He collapsed the cup in the palm of his hand then opened it again. "Astonishing." He passed the cup to Angela and crouched down, poking through the growing pile. "Hey, this could be useful." He held up two packages. "Green tea and little sesame seed munchies."

Erin looked up at him with a smile. "There are some protein bars in there somewhere too."

Bill made a face.

"Don't knock it, they just might come in handy." She turned her attention back to unpacking and pulled out the familiar white box with the red cross. "Finally. Here's the first aid kit."

"I don't really need that, you know." Gray pulled on his T-shirt, eyeing her warily as she folded the fabric for a sling.

"Of course you do," she replied briskly. "Besides, the sooner you're able to use your arm the better." She adjusted the sling around his neck. "There," she said, "doesn't that ease the pressure on your shoulder?"

He nodded reluctantly. "Yeah, it does."

"How's the pain?" she asked quietly, picking up his jacket. Bill and Angela were exclaiming over the treasures in her duffel bag. "There are some pain pills in the kit."

"Maybe later," he said, allowing her to slip the jacket over his shoulders. "I want a clear head for the next few hours. We need to make ourselves some sort of a shelter and collect firewood." He scanned up and down the beach then his gaze came back to rest on her face. "And we need to find some fresh water. I'll help as much as I can, but you'll have to do most of the heavy lifting." Her looked at her steadily. "But I have a feeling you're used to that." He reached out with his good arm and tilted up her chin. "Aren't you?"

Her throat tightened and her eyes stung as tears welled up, threatening to spill over. She opened her mouth to speak, but no words came out. Blinking rapidly, she turned aside. With Gray temporarily incapacitated, Bill's heart condition and Angela's hands in blisters, it was important for her to remain strong. She knew that, but just once she'd like to sit back and allow someone else to be in charge. The idea was so foreign to her, so far-fetched, that she almost laughed out loud. Instead, she reached deep down inside and pulled herself together. "Just let me take care of Angela's hands, and we'll get organized." She lowered her voice again.

"Maybe you could check on Bill. All of this stress can't be good for his heart."

Angela watched stoically as Erin spread a thin coating of antibiotic ointment on her raw skin and bound her hands with gauze. "I can still help around here," she stated when Erin had finished. "Tell me what you'd like me to do."

"I'd rather you didn't get your bandages dirty. The roll of gauze isn't all that big." Erin nodded toward the items from her bag. "Would you mind going through the rest of my things and seeing what we might be able to use? I have no idea how long we're going to be here, but we should be prepared."

Angela lowered her voice. "I've been trying not to think about it. You know, about how long we might be stuck here." She glanced back at Gray and Bill. "Has our captain said anything to you? Do you know if he got a chance make a distress call?"

"That's the problem. The power shorted out, and there was no way he could contact anyone." Erin looked down at the small pile of her belongings. "What are the odds? None of us has a cell phone. Gray is the only one who uses one and he left it for his business." She rolled her eyes. "I hate the things, but right now I'm wishing I'd kept mine."

"And I'm wishing I hadn't left mine at home. Woulda, shoulda, coulda." Angela crossed her arms over her chest. "How about we make a fire? Maybe someone will spot us from a passing boat."

"It's a possibility." Erin looked back toward the islands, and the open sea beyond. "You know those islands are both a blessing and a curse. They might prevent someone from spotting us, but at the same time they'll shelter us if a storm comes up."

"But the smoke from the fire . . ." Angela's voice trailed off.

"What is it?" Erin could see thoughts moving behind her friend's eyes.

"I was just remembering what Bill said this morning. How the mist hanging in the trees looks just like smoke." She turned to Erin, her expression grim. "Most ships stay well out in the deeper water, so if anyone spots us it'll be dumb luck. Seems to me that when we're rescued it will be as a result of a search, so let's try to figure out when we might be missed. I'm surprising Danny, so he's not expecting me."

Erin nodded. "And I'm not due to arrive for two weeks." She paused. "Well, twelve days from today. But they're not expecting me, either."

"And Bill told me he had an open invitation." Angela looked over at Gray. "So that leaves Gray, and the boat. Hopefully The Lodge is expecting his delivery." She grabbed Erin's arm. "Come on, let's go ask him."

"Well, sort of." Gray settled down in the sand, his back against one of the logs. They had naturally gravitated to the shelter of the logs. "Ben keeps them well-supplied with fuel, so they probably won't start wondering about him 'till they start running low."

"So we're on our own." Angela's voice quavered, and she quickly held up her bandaged hands to ward off any comments. "No, it's okay. Erin and I already figured that out, but it's starting to sink in, that's all." She looked up at the sky. Wispy clouds had covered the sun again and a chill breeze swept in from the ocean. "I'm going to finish sorting through Erin's stuff to see what we can use and then I'll help collect firewood." She forced a bright smile. "After all, a fire is still our best hope of being spotted fairly soon."

"I'll start collecting firewood." Bill had been leaning against one of the logs. "And while I'm at it, I'll keep an eye out for thin poles we might use to put a roof over our shelter."

Erin pointed to a rocky outcrop near the tree line. "I thought I'd see if there are any loose rocks up there and bring them down here to make a firepit."

He flexed the fingers of his right hand. "I've still got one good arm. I'll clear away a patch of sand where we're going to build the fire." He swiveled his head, scanning the piles of logs. "Maybe I can find a flat piece of wood to use."

"I've got it." Erin ran to the inflatable. "Use one of these coffee cans. Then we can use them to boil water. Assuming we can find some, that is."

Gray pointed to the north end of the beach, half a mile distant. "Bill and I both think there's a stream running into the ocean over there. Let's get this firepit built and we can go for a walk."

Erin pried out the largest rocks she could handle while Gray dug a sizeable hole in the sand for the firepit. It felt good to be doing something positive.

"Can you find one that's flat on one side?" asked Gray, shoving her most recent delivery into place. "We could set the can of hot water on it when it's boiled."

"Hey, Gray!" Bill dumped a load of dry wood beside the firepit. "There's some sort of a metal grate back there." He pointed to a pile of logs. "Looks like it came from a barbecue or something. Just about rusted through in the middle, but I think we could use a corner of it to support the coffee can when we're boiling water."

"Let's have a look." Gray rose enthusiastically. "Probably left by someone who had a fire here."

When Erin staggered back carrying a flat-sided rock, Gray and Bill had managed to firmly wedge the metal rack into place. "See?" said Bill with a boyish grin. "It may not be a professional kitchen, but at least we're innovative."

"It's wonderful." Erin dropped the rock in the remaining space. "I can already taste that first cup of tea. Those silly cups will come in handy after all." She raised her head. "Now what's she doing?"

Angela was grunting with the effort of rolling a short section of log with her foot. Evenly sawn, it was almost pure white, as were most of the logs that littered the beach above the water line. "It's for Bill," she panted, clearing a level space and placing it upright beside the firepit. She looked shyly at the older man. "I noticed that you didn't like getting down on the sand and I thought you could use this as a stool."

"Well, well." Bill was visibly moved. "That's very thoughtful of you, my dear." He promptly sat down and beamed at the small circle of faces. "While I was collecting firewood I spotted several poles that are small enough to drag over here." He rose and indicated the two logs that formed the sides of their shelter. "If we place them up here, on top of these logs, they'll support our roof. Without a roof the mist will chill us right through at night, even if it doesn't rain. Between the two of us, Gray and I can manage some, and if she isn't wiped out from carrying those rocks, maybe Erin could handle a couple as well."

"Let's do it." Erin was suddenly energized. "It beats sitting around worrying about when we're going to be found."

The poles went up very quickly. Erin found some battered and broken sheets of plywood along the shoreline and hauled them out onto the sand to be brought back later. Angela finished sorting through Erin's bag then joined in the search, pouncing on several one-gallon plastic containers, brittle from exposure to the elements but still serviceable.

"Isn't it silly?" she said to Erin as they stopped to catch their breath. "At home we live with so many luxuries, so many gadgets, and here we get excited over finding an old metal screen and a couple of plastic milk jugs. Sort of puts things in perspective, huh?" She pushed her hair out of her eyes. "Even so, I was glad to find some matches in your duffel bag."

"Matches?" Erin frowned. "Oh, that's right. Another of the gifts I thought was foolish. Thank goodness for waterproof containers."

"Amen." Angela nodded to herself then turned to Erin. "We're going to be all right, aren't we? I mean, somebody's going to come looking for us soon, aren't they?"

Erin couldn't bring herself to lie. She pulled her friend down on one of the smaller logs. "Yes, we are going to be found, but as I said before, I honestly don't know when. In the meantime, we're going to do just fine." She looked back at their makeshift shelter. "We are four intelligent, capable people and so far there hasn't been a moment's conflict. How unusual is that? I mean, look at what you did for Bill, bringing him that piece of log to sit on." She put her arm around Angela's shoulders. "That was so sweet."

"That was easy." Angela pulled back, eyes shimmering with tears. "I wish I could be strong like you. I don't mean strong like hauling rocks. I mean mentally. How do you do it?"

Erin picked up a handful of sand then let it spill through her fingers and sift gently back down onto the beach. "This is my kind of thing," she said, speaking almost to herself. "It's what I've always done, getting things organized, getting people to work together." She gave a soft chuckle and Angela looked at her curiously. "A kitchen can be a war zone. As an executive chef a big part of my job is to ensure that everyone works together to make it run smoothly. At least here we all like each other."

Angela nodded slowly.

Erin continued. "And we all have different strengths. You're sensitive to other people's feelings, I'm good at organizing, Bill is steady as a rock, and Gray . . . well, I'm not sure yet exactly what Gray brings to the table."

"I notice you two are getting along a lot better."

Erin couldn't help but smile. "You noticed, huh?"

She kicked at the sand, lost in thought. "That first morning, before you arrived, he acted as though he hated me. It was the strangest thing."

"Well I don't know what you did to change his mind, but I've caught him looking at you a couple of times." Angela grinned knowingly. "He doesn't hate you now."

"You really think so?" Erin heard the eagerness in her voice, but she didn't care.

"Honey, when you're around he can't take his eyes off you."

"But I'm . . ." Erin waved her hands in the air. "I'm not his type."

"How do you know that? How do you know what kind of woman he likes?"

"Oh, come on Angela. He's gorgeous, in case you haven't noticed." She gave a delicate little shudder. "He's got that quiet aura of authority about him that's like catnip to most women. And those eyes! Have you noticed how . . ." She stood up abruptly. "I'm being ridiculous. Don't listen to me."

"Are you kidding? You were just getting warmed up." Angela jumped up and brushed the sand from the seat of her slacks. "Don't stop now."

Erin turned to her friend. "It's just that I like him, okay? I like him and I don't want to get my hopes up. I'll go off to my new job at The Lodge and he'll go back to being a pilot." She managed to find a grip on an ungainly piece of plywood. "Come on, let's go back and see what the guys are up to."

With Gray's help she managed to slide the piece of plywood up onto the cross poles. "There are a couple more pieces like this back there," she said, standing back to admire their efforts. "Where do you think they come from, anyway?"

"Could be anywhere. Especially when you think about all the ships that go up and down this coast." He shielded his eyes and looked out between the islands. The ocean looked cold and forbidding in the pale sunlight. "I've talked to some of the old hands along this coast—most of them fishermen—and they tell me that as recently as thirty or forty years ago it was fairly common to find glass floats from Japanese fishing nets along these shores. Those pieces of plywood look like they were in the water for a while. Probably washed overboard from a freighter." He adjusted the sling. "Come on, let's get the other pieces."

When they returned with two more misshapen pieces of plywood they found Bill seated on his log, using Gray's pocket knife to rip fine pieces of wood from a small chunk of driftwood. He looked up as they man-handled the sheets into place and Erin was relieved to see that his unhealthy pallor was gone, and that there was a definite sparkle in his eyes. "Angela and I were just saying how much we'd enjoy a cup of tea." He wiggled his eyebrows. "And in case you were wondering, that's a hint." A long, curled shaving of wood joined the others in a pile at his feet. "If you two would go and get some water, we'll have a fire going by the time you get back."

"How are you holding up?" They were walking side by side on the hard-packed sand, Gray carrying the coffee cans and Erin carrying the plastic containers.

"Me?" She played for time, unsure of how to respond. "Okay I guess." It was disconcerting when he looked at her like that, as though he really cared. She gestured ahead, trying to change the focus of his attention. "It's a good-sized stream. We're lucky."

"In more ways than one. It's a perfect size. Big enough for our needs, but not so large that it will attract bears. They love to fish at the mouth of the big rivers, especially where they've deposited silt over the years, creating an estuary."

Erin stopped walking. "I hadn't thought of that." She glanced back toward their campsite. "Don't mention bears to Angela, okay? She's being awfully brave, but deep down she's scared."

"And you're not?" He drew his brows together, at least what was left of them.

She gave him a quick, searching look. "Should I be? Somehow I've been too busy to worry about much of anything." She started walking again. "It's a good thing we don't have a mirror."

"Oh, why is that?"

A laugh bubbled up in her throat and she looked away. "Because your eyelashes are little stubs, and your eyebrows are almost gone."

"Really?" A thoughtful look came over his face as he ran his fingers along the ridge of his brow, exploring the unfamiliar terrain. Continuing the exploration, he rubbed the backs of his fingers along the line of his jaw. The sound was raspy and masculine and it raised little goosebumps on Erin's arms. Her stomach clenched, and she inhaled sharply, trying not to let him see how she'd been affected by the simple, unconscious gesture. Her legendary composure was in tatters and once again she ached to reach out and touch him.

Unaware of her reaction, Gray glanced at his watch. "It's four o'clock. What time was it when the explosion happened? Around ten, wasn't it?" Erin nodded. "Somehow it doesn't seem possible." He touched his brow again, and gave his head a quick, disbelieving shake. "It seems like it happened in another lifetime."

They had come to the edge of the stream. Over time it had carved out a shallow valley and a short distance upstream a fallen tree had created a dam with a large pool behind it. Water spilled over the dam, burbling gently on its way to mix with the salt water of the ocean.

"I'll rinse out the containers and fill them." Erin slid down the side of the bank and made her way along a shoreline of small pebbles. Within minutes she had filled the jugs and partially filled the coffee cans. Her leg muscles protested as she climbed out of the creek bottom. Their campsite appeared miles away, almost as though she was looking at it through the wrong end of her binoculars. For the first time that day she admitted to herself that she was tired. Working in a kitchen required stamina, but hauling rocks and trudging on the beach demanded a different sort of energy.

"You don't have to carry both of those cans, you know." He was struggling with them, trying to balance one against his chest with the injured arm while he held the other in his right hand. "One can will do, along with these jugs."

"No, no. I'll be all right." His reply was needlessly

sharp, jarring Erin for a moment. He paused to adjust the cans, and she continued walking, hurt but proud of herself for not reacting. It took a moment for her to realize he'd stopped. She turned slowly, watching him struggle.

"Sorry." He gave her a rueful smile. "You're the last person I should be sniping at." His voice rang with sincerity. "You're right. We don't need all this water." He poured the contents of one of the cans in the sand and repositioned the other. "I feel useless, that's all." He caught up with her, smiled, and her heart melted.

He studied her for several heartbeats. "You're not going to let me get away with anything, are you?" He cocked his head to one side, waiting for her response.

"Not for a minute." She smiled back at him. "Come on, they're waiting."

Gray smelled the smoke before he saw it. Drifting toward them on the breeze, it reminded him of his childhood, of hot summer afternoons at the beach. Lazy, carefree days spent examining tidal pools, or building sandcastles with his friends, then destroying them gleefully amid furious battles between opposing armies. Back then, in those sun-drenched days, his parents had been happy. At least they had seemed happy. It wasn't until later that he started to sense the tension between them, to hear the angry voices that stopped abruptly when he entered the room. One scene in particular was as clear to him now as if it had happened yesterday. His father turning his back, stiff with tension while his mother stood beside the fireplace, a brittle smile on her face and a glass of sherry in her hand.

"They've got the fire started." Erin's voice broke into his thoughts. "I can see the smoke."

Her eyes lit up as she spoke, and she lengthened her stride. Gray quickened his pace. He wasn't normally a tea drinker, but today the prospect of any sort of hot drink gave him the added impetus to keep up. He glanced sideways at the woman beside him. She'd twisted her hair into some sort of a braid earlier this morning, but wisps of hair had worked loose all over her head, a soft nimbus of rich brown shot through with flashes of golden red. The braid bounced against her back with every step and he was almost overcome by a desire to loosen it and run his fingers through those thick, glossy strands. His thoughts drifted back to his former girlfriend. Holly had discouraged him from touching her hair, claiming that she'd worked hard to '*get it perfect*'. He looked at Erin again. There was nothing superficial about her. It was a comforting thought. Not comforting like an old pair of jeans that you hated to throw away. No, he thought, sneaking another glance in her direction. Comforting in the way of old friends who enjoyed spending time together without the need to talk every moment. But who was he kidding? Once they were found, his life was going to get crazy. He needed to make a decision on the purchase of another aircraft for his business and Erin would be immersed in her new job. She wouldn't give him a second thought. Or would she? He was surprised to discover that he wanted to know the answer to that question.

Chapter Six

Erin sank down onto the sand, grateful for a chance to rest. Surrounded by the circle of rocks, the fire crackled happily, radiating warmth throughout their makeshift shelter. Now she understood why Gray had insisted on digging down about a foot. Very little heat was lost and as a result the sand around the edges of the fire was already heating up. She took off her running shoes and socks and wiggled her feet in the warm sand, sighing with pleasure.

"Listen to this!" Angela sat cross-legged, Erin's book on edible plants in her lap. "It's about kelp, of which there are many kinds." She looked up, making sure that she had everyone's attention. "A one hundred gram portion contains one thousand ninety-five milligrams of calcium, two hundred and forty milligrams of phosphorus, approximately three thousand milligrams of sodium and five thousand two hundred and fifty of potassium." She closed the book and looked up triumphantly. "And that's just for starters." Using the book, she gestured toward the forest. "A person couldn't starve around here if they tried. There are any number of edible plants, and lots of fruit in season."

Gray placed the coffee can of water on the grate and settled down beside Bill. "You're absolutely right. Our First Nations people lived very well along this coast. Anthropologists like to point out that the reason they produced so many beautiful carvings and other art forms is that they didn't have to spend all their time searching for food."

Angela brandished the book. "I can see why." She turned to Bill, who was whittling on a slender piece of driftwood with Gray's knife. "What are you working on now?"

"I'm making a stick for digging clams." He held up the end of a piece of driftwood for inspection. The carved end resembled a shoehorn. "Not the traditional shape, but it's better than trying to use our hands." Holding the stick like a pointer, be directed their attention to the rocks on the southern end of the beach. "And over there, on those rocks, are enough mussels to feed us for a month. I checked it out with my binoculars, and I've been watching the tide, which is on the way out."

Angela pushed herself up. "Mussels? I love mussels!" She clapped her hands in childlike glee. "I'll gladly collect them if our chef will cook them." She turned to Erin. "Would you?"

"Sure, I'll give it a try." Her friend's enthusiasm was contagious. "By rights we should have some white wine, but water will do for steaming. And since there's such a plentiful supply, I'd also like to try wrapping them in kelp leaves and throwing them in the fire." She warmed to her subject. "The worst thing that can happen is that we cook them too long and they get tough. But I think a few minutes should do it." She gazed around at the circle of faces. "I'd forgotten all about food. Sorry about that."

"Don't be ridiculous. It's not your responsibility. But I like your idea of using kelp, and there's plenty of it strewn along the high tide mark." Bill peered into the coffee can. "Looks like the water's boiling. Let's have that tea now."

Angela passed around the cups of steaming liquid and the group fell into a comfortable silence.

"Snacks!" Angela turned to Erin. "Do you think we could have one of those sesame seed snacks now?"

"Of course, of course." Erin waved toward the small pile of her possessions. "And please don't think you have to ask. From now on, what's there belongs to all of us."

Angela opened the sesame snacks and handed one piece to each person. "Don't forget your pills," she said to Bill, fussing over the older man with obvious enjoyment.

Erin nibbled on the sesame snack, scarcely aware of the sweetness on her taste buds. What she'd said earlier was true. She hadn't thought about food since breakfast. Gray was right—it did seem like another lifetime. She wasn't sure she could put it into words, but deep inside her something was different. Sipping at the tea, she stared into the dancing flames. Today's events, as horrific as they had been, had changed her in ways she didn't quite understand. For a few frantic hours she hadn't thought about being overweight, or about Crystal. She'd acted on instinct, free of her usual self-doubt, and it felt good. A piece of wood exploded in a shower of sparks, as though heralding the future. And the future looked very promising indeed.

"That was perfectly adequate." Bill patted his stomach appreciatively. Erin had watched him eat a few mussels and could tell that he hadn't enjoyed them as much as he professed.

"How about a protein bar for dessert?" She removed the foil wrap and handed it to him. He couldn't very well refuse it now. "Anyone else?" She held up another one, and Gray and Angela both shook their head. She returned it to the package and sat down again. The clouds along the horizon glowed faintly with the last rays of the sun. "We appear to have everything we need for tonight." A large pile of driftwood was positioned just outside the shelter. She looked around at the others. At Erin's insistence, Angela was using the sleeping bag from her duffel bag. The slender blond would be the first to feel the chill of the night air. The three slickers would make excellent ground sheets and makeshift blankets for the rest of them.

Erin lay down and patted the warm sand. She squirmed around, making a comfortable hollow for her hip. "I just can't stay awake any longer," she murmured, groggy from the stress of the day and the warmth of the fire. "Goodnight everyone."

"Goodnight Erin." Three voices chorused back at her, but she'd already drifted away.

Pale light filtered in through the tree roots. Erin opened her eyes, and it took her a moment to remember where she was. Strange . . . her back was warm, but the rest of her body was slightly chilled. She must have rolled over during the night. Feeling for her watch, she brought it up close to her face, peering at it myopically. Five forty-five. She rolled over, painfully aware of every muscle in her body. Movement was difficult, and she realized that she was tangled in the slicker. Needing to be free of the constricting garment she tore at the snaps. They sounded like cannon fire in the silence and she paused, looking around to see if she'd woken anyone else. The others were still sleeping soundly, and she slipped the slicker over her head, glad to be free of the voluminous folds. Embers still burned at the bottom of the fire pit, and she added a few pieces of driftwood, watching as the fire came to life, flames licking greedily at the wood. Moving about silently in the soft sand, she picked up the slicker and went out to greet the morning.

The tide was fully out, revealing rocky outcrops containing small tidal pools. There hadn't been time to check them out last night, and she made a promise to herself to explore them today. She could happily spend hours watching tiny fish dart around, or tiny hermit crabs scuttle across the bottom in their constant search for food. Overhead, the sky was achingly blue and she said a silent prayer, grateful that the weather seemed to be co-operating. A gentle breeze lifted a strand of hair, tossing it into her eyes. Brushing it away impatiently, she looked back toward the shelter. She had a hairbrush in with her personal items, but that could wait. She loosened the tie that held her braid and raked through her hair with her fingers. It felt good, and she faced into the breeze, enjoying the sensation of freedom, and of being alone. She looked around with new eyes. The sheltered bay with rocky headlands at either end was breathtakingly beautiful. They had been perversely lucky to be thrown up on this beach. She wandered idly along, mentally reviewing yesterday's events. It was surprising how easily they'd worked together. As a group they had coped remarkably well, and she knew with confidence that they could manage for as long as necessary.

She slipped down into the sand, resting her back against a log. She'd promised herself that she would think about her relationship with her sister, but suddenly that didn't seem important any more. When had she stopped feeling responsible for Crystal's behavior? She didn't know, but it was about time. She'd done the best job she knew how. She may have spoiled her, given her too much attention, but ultimately her sister would have to decide what kind of a person she wanted to be.

The sun's rays gilded the tips of the trees on the islands. Erin wrapped her arms around her knees and watched the golden light slide down through the branches. A crow landed on the beach not far in front of her, picking through the seaweed that had washed up overnight. It took a startled hop backwards and seemed to be looking past her shoulder. Then it took to the air, landing farther along the beach.

"This is my favorite time of day." Gray slumped awkwardly down on the sand beside her and looked up at the sky. "Anything seems possible." He swung his good arm, taking in the sky from horizon to horizon. "A clean slate, as it were."

Erin shot him a quizzical look. "Are you all right this morning? You're talking in clichés."

He turned and gave her a lazy smile, eyes glowing like living pieces of lapis lazuli. "Yeah, I guess I am." Reaching out, he brushed the back of his fingers against her cheek and a jolt of electricity flashed through her body. She wondered if he could feel her pulse throbbing under her skin.

"Sand," he said softly, skewering her with an intense gaze. "You had a bit of sand on your cheek."

"Oh." She raised a hand, touching her cheek. Odd . . . it didn't seem to be on fire!

"Anyway," he continued, leaning back against the log again, "I like mornings." He slanted a look in her direction. "I do my best work in the mornings."

She nodded, afraid to trust her voice. Did he have any idea what he was doing to her? She swallowed hard, fighting for composure.

He gave a contented sigh, and she chanced a look in his direction. He seemed satisfied to watch the progress of the sun as it illuminated the offshore islands and worked across the water toward their position. It was already banishing the chill from the air.

"Under the circumstances this probably sounds crazy, but I can't think of anywhere I'd rather be right now." His eyes took on a faraway look. "Although a cup of coffee would be nice."

"I'd like a hot shower." The words were out before she knew it. She toyed with her hair band. "Well I would!"

"I believe you." He rolled his head back against the log, eyes closed. Erin studied the dark smudges under his eyes, evidence of the strain he'd been under since yesterday. "If I had the Mallard I'd take you to a place you'd never forget." He opened one eye to see if she was listening. "It's oh, about a hundred miles north. Right on the coast, a few miles from the inlet where The Lodge is presently anchored." The tension drained from his face as he spoke. "It's a series of hot pools fed by a thermal spring that comes out of the ground up on the side of the hill. Over the years, the minerals in the water have created these extraordinary pools. They're almost perfect circles, and one spills into the other, all the way down to the sea." His hand illustrated the various levels, and she could almost see it as he spoke. "On a cold day you can see the steam rising from about a mile away. All the commercial fishermen know about the pools, but seldom use them."

"It sounds wonderful." Erin turned toward him, relaxing against the log. "Are they hot?"

"Very." He raised an eyebrow, a silent challenge. "It's not called the Rim of Fire for nothing."

Erin acknowledged his point with a shrug of her

shoulders. "I suppose not. So the lower the pool, the cooler the temperature?"

"Exactly right and I'll tell you what. I promised you a plane ride so why don't we make it to the hot pools? Soak away our aches and pains and talk over old times?"

It sounded heavenly. "I'd enjoy that. A lot." The mention of the future brought her back to earth with a thud. "In the meantime, I was wondering if there's anything else we should be doing to draw attention to ourselves. Like spell out H-E-L-P with logs. Does that sound too corny?"

"Not at all." He smacked himself in the head with the heel of his hand. "I should have thought of that myself."

Erin reached for his hand and pulled it down. "Give yourself a break, Gray. As a matter of fact, I'm glad you didn't think of it. I couldn't have done another thing yesterday." She realized that she was holding his hand, and made to let go but he grasped it tightly and brought it to his lips. His beard scratched the backs of her fingers, but it was softer than she'd imagined it to be.

"You were great yesterday." He released her hand and she took it back reluctantly. "You held us all together."

"Did I?" She thought back to her actions of the previous day. They didn't seem out of the ordinary.

"Bill and I were talking about how nothing seemed to bother you."

"Speaking of Bill . . ." she quickly changed the subject. "I'm not sure if you noticed, but he didn't eat much last night. He only had a few mussels. Not enough for someone recovering from bypass surgery."

"I didn't realize it until you almost forced that protein bar on him." His eyes softened. "That was nice of you, Erin. He's very special to me."

"That's right, he told me he's your godfather. Did have you seen much of him growing up?"

He kicked at the sand, seemingly lost in thought. "When I was younger, he was around a lot. But when my parents split up Uncle Bill and Aunt Chloe seemed to drift away. It was never the same after that."

"So he's married? He hasn't mentioned his wife. Chloe, is it?"

"She died six or seven years ago. Great lady, but she smoked a couple of packs a day. By the time they diagnosed lung cancer, she only had a few more months to live. He was devastated, of course. Thank goodness their children live nearby. Jen—that's his daughter—wanted him to stay there for a few weeks, but his grandchildren are teenagers and they can get pretty noisy. I think that's part of the reason he wants to go to The Lodge."

"And he gets this instead."

"True, but you know I think in a way he's enjoying it. Why wouldn't he? Angela fusses over him like a mother hen, and you watch everything he eats. What's not to like?"

"You called him Uncle. Is he related to one of your parents?"

He shook his head. "No, it just sort of happened."

"We had the same thing when we were younger. Good friends of my parents. I still call them Aunt Joan and Uncle Ernie." She fell silent for a moment, lost in memories.

The sun rose higher, and the shadow of the trees behind them retreated up the beach. Gray stretched and, using his good arm, pushed himself to his feet. "We'll need some more water this morning." He held out his hand, offering to pull her up. "Feel like a walk?"

She took his hand and he effortlessly pulled her to her feet. It was strange, but around him she didn't feel clumsy and overweight, the way she did around most men. Maybe it was the way he looked at her. Well, perhaps not in the beginning, but the man who stood beside her now was different from the one she'd met two mornings ago. She studied him openly. He was softer around the edges now—easier to approach.

"See something you like?" His voice was low and throaty and she took a step backward, stunned by her body's instantaneous response to his words. Every nerve ending in her body sizzled and her heart was beating double time. Not for the first time she wondered if he had any idea what effect he was having on her. She grabbed the rain slicker from the log and proceeded to fold it, over and over, until it was as small as she could manage. She was stalling for time—she knew it and he knew it, but he waited while she composed herself.

"Why are you doing this to me?" she blurted, regretting the words the moment they were uttered.

Now it was his turn to step back. "Hey, I was only teasing . . ."

Teasing? Tears sprang up instantly, burning the back of her eyes but she held them back. She'd never let him see how much he'd hurt her with those words. She whirled around and started back toward the shelter.

"Erin!" Gray caught up to her and grabbed her arm. "What did I say?" He hunched his shoulders and gave his head a quick, confused shake. His eyes searched hers. "We were getting along so well . . ." His voice drifted off.

He released her arm, breaking the connection between them. How could she have been so foolish as to think he was beginning to care for her? In the blink of an eye all the old insecurities had come flooding back.

"Don't mind me," she said lightly, forcing a smile into her voice. "And you're right, we're getting along just fine." She nodded her head, adding emphasis to her words. "Come on, let's go and get that water."

He handed her one of the water jugs and fell into step beside her. "I hope you don't mind," he said, fumbling in his pocket, "but I brought this with me. You said that everything in that pile was for our use." He held out a small box, the cardboard dark and brittle with age. "It's the Popiel Pocket Fisherman."

"And you thought . . ."

"Yeah." He broke into a grin. "I thought we might be able to catch a fish or two. Bill loves fish and there should be some good sized trout in that pond behind the weir." His enthusiasm was infectious. "The pool goes back quite a way and there are trees and shrubs growing out over the edge. Perfect habitat."

Erin's mouth started to water, and she realized that

she'd scarcely eaten in the past twenty-four hours. One sesame cracker and a few mussels, to be exact. "A trout would make a fine breakfast," she said, and felt herself relaxing.

Gray put a finger to his lips as they approached the pool. Wispy strands of mist rose from the surface, and much of it was still in the shadow of the trees. "Do you mind waiting 'till later to fill the jugs? I'll make my way around through the woods. Sneak up on them, as it were." He looked up through the trees. "This is the perfect time of day. Now and at dusk. So if you'd just find a quiet space to sit for a while, I'll see if this baby works." He jiggled the strange contraption in his hand. "Doesn't look like any fishing pole I've ever seen, but let's give it a whirl."

Erin found a comfortable spot and by the time she was settled, Gray had disappeared in the woods. She held her breath, waiting for him to reappear. He'd said there were probably no bears around, but she wasn't sure if that was true or if he'd been trying to calm her fears. She fought back the warm feeling that threatened to overwhelm her. No! She couldn't allow herself to think of him like that. He was only being nice to her because she knew David Kendall, and he wanted to continue flying customers up to The Lodge.

He appeared halfway down the pool and her thoughts returned to The Lodge. She'd seen pictures, done the virtual tour on line, and made her decision to accept David's offer on that basis. He'd offered to fly her up, to let her inspect 'her' new kitchen, but she'd been too busy. Now she wished she'd been more cautious. David had assured her that he would modify the kitchen in any way she requested, but she wasn't concerned about that. It was the people she'd be working with that made her wish she'd been more cautious. Would they be professionals? Her standards were high, and in an operation that was seasonal, she wondered how The Lodge could attract and hold skilled people.

Lost in thought, she didn't notice that Gray's first cast had been successful until the fish leaped out of the water. It wasn't a classic battle between man and fish, but that didn't dull her excitement. The fish jumped again, writhing and twisting at the end of the line; caught for a moment in a shaft of sunlight. Then it plunged back into the dark green pool and Gray shuffled sideways along the shoreline, the expression on his face alternating between triumph and terror. He struggled to reel in the fish with the awkward piece of equipment, but even across the pond she sensed his resolve to land the fish. That was what she liked about him—he was unwilling to give up. At that moment he bent over and reeled furiously. The fish came out of the water and he straightened, almost losing his balance but grinning broadly.

"You did it!" Erin stood up and clapped. "Bravo."

He made a clumsy bow, bending over his injured arm while the fish dangled from the other hand, still twisting at the end of the line. "Breakfast of champions," he shouted, making his way along the edge of the pool. Part way along he picked up a piece of wood and rapped the fish on the head. "Sorry," he said as he got closer. "But the

darned thing was going to jump right out of my hand."
He held it up for her inspection, one finger through the
gills. "Steelhead. About twelve pounds, I think."

"It's beautiful," she said, fingering the iridescent
scales. The hook was still caught in the corner of the
mouth. "Shall I take the hook out?" She gestured to his
arm in the sling. "Kind of hard for you to manage with
that, I imagine."

"You don't mind?" He raised his eyebrows.

"I'm a chef, remember? I'll clean it too, if you have
your knife with you." She gave the hook a sharp twist,
pulling it out.

"I do, as a matter of fact. Come on." He slid down
the bank and laid the fish on the rocks. "I'll sort out our
little fishing rod while you work."

Erin opened the knife, got a firm grip on the fish and
slit it open. Yanking out the guts and organs with a few
quick, efficient movements she looked up to find him
watching her with a bemused smile on his face. "What?"
she challenged. "Never seen a woman clean a fish?"

"Actually, no." His eyes followed her movements as
she ran her finger along the spine, cleaning out the last
of the blood. "You're amazing."

"Yeah, well you were pretty amazing yourself." She
didn't know what else to say. She rinsed the fish in the
stream. The seagulls would finish cleaning up the mess
soon enough. They were already hopping toward them
on the sand, their raucous cries shrill in her ears.

Erin rinsed off the knife, dried it carefully on the
bottom of her T-shirt and handed it back to Gray with
the fish. "I'll get the water and we can head back."

They trudged along the sand in comfortable silence. He was easy to be with, and she was regretting her earlier outburst. But maybe it had been for the best. After all, her trust in a man had been shattered once this year. She didn't want to try for twice.

"I'll wrap the fish in that," she said, pointing to a glistening pile of seaweed just ahead. "I can taste it now. I'll bet that even The Lodge won't be serving anything better for breakfast this morning."

Chapter Seven

"**K**endall here." David Kendall picked up the telephone in his home office. "Oh hello, Connor. How are things at the Lodge?" He listened to the lodge manager for a few moments. "The new chef? I couldn't really say. She was taking a couple of weeks off between jobs so she could be anywhere." An eagle flew by with a fish in its talons, headed toward a nearby nest. It was one of the joys of living at Deep Cove. He gave his head a quick shake, forcing himself to concentrate on the conversation. A problem with the produce for The Lodge required a change in supplier, and the current chef had recommended that Erin be allowed to choose her own supplier. He nodded his head in agreement. "That's good thinking. Listen, I have her home number around here somewhere. Why don't I call her and ask her to get in touch with you." He made a dismissive motion with his hand. "No, don't worry about it. I'd like the chance to touch base with her again anyway." He disconnected and stood looking out the window, lost in thought. He'd been fortunate that Erin had agreed to take the position. He'd try to find out when she planned to arrive at The Lodge, and ask Connor to set up an informal get-together with the rest of the staff.

Checking his list of contacts on the computer he found her name and dialed her home number. The phone rang several times and he was about to hang up when a childlike voice answered.

"Hello?"

This wasn't the woman he remembered! He checked the phone number again. "Is this Erin Delaney?"

The phone clattered in his ear as though someone had dropped it. After a moment's fumbling the voice was back. "No, it's Crystal."

He frowned, and looked at the piece of paper again. "Is this five, five, five, three, seven, seven, six?"

"Yes, but Erin isn't here. This is Crystal Delaney."

"Could you give me a number where she can be reached?"

"No. What time is it?"

David looked at his watch. "Seven forty-five."

"Oh my gosh. I should have been up ages ago."

"Listen, it's rather important that I contact Erin. Do you know where she is?"

"She's gone off to some fishing lodge up the coast." The breathy voice gathered strength. "I don't know why. She had a perfectly good job here."

David suppressed a sharp retort. "How long ago did she leave?"

"What? Oh, I don't know. Four days, maybe five. I mean she didn't even fly up like a regular person. She went up on some silly boat." She stopped abruptly. "Seven forty-five did you say? Oh no, I'm going to be late for work." The connection was abruptly broken and David stared into the handset. "And good-bye to you, too Miss Crystal."

He re-connected with The Lodge and his manager. "Connor, do you know when the supply boat is due? Evidently our new chef decided to come early, and she's on it."

"Really? That's great, but I'm afraid I can't help you. They've never been on a fixed schedule, but since Ben Millar took over they've been coming once a week. I was away at that seminar last week, so I don't know what day they came. Would you like me to find out for you?"

"No need. I'll call Ben's company and see what they can tell me." He gave an audible sigh. "Too bad she's one of those people who detests cell phones. They make life so much easier."

"You've got that right. Anyway I'll hope to hear from her today. I'll leave you to track her down."

"Skookum Charters. Ben speaking."

"Ben? It's David Kendall. What are you doing there? I thought you were on the way to The Lodge."

"Oh, hello, Mr. Kendall. I'd sure like to be on the boat, but I broke my leg last week."

"Is it serious?"

"No, but I'd only be a liability on the water, so my

friends who know enough about running the coastline are filling in for me until I can get back at it."

"That's good. You're a lucky man to have friends like that." He became more businesslike. "Listen, while I have you on the phone I'd like to check on a couple of things. Our new chef may be on the current trip. Does that ring any bells?"

"I think so. What was his name again?"

"It's a female. And her name is Erin Delaney."

Ben grabbed the clipboard that hung beside his desk. "Uh-oh."

"I'm not sure I like the sound of that. What does 'uh-oh' mean?"

Ben spoke quickly. "Nothing serious, sir. It's just that I had her down as A-a-r-o-n. I don't know where the mix-up occurred, but I assumed it was a man."

"Don't worry, I'm sure she gets that a lot. And while we're at it, I'm also expecting an old friend some time soon and I'm wondering if he's on the same boat. His name's Bill Corbett. William."

"Sounds familiar." Ben flipped the sheets of paper. "Corbett. Yes, here he is. Called a couple of days before they left."

David smiled to himself. "Great. So when did they leave? Or better yet, when will they be arriving?"

Ben glanced automatically at his watch. "Should be arriving around noon today, but we've never kept to a strict schedule, so it could be later. I could try to raise them on the radio if you like."

"No, never mind." David made a quick decision. "Sounds like Bill's trying to surprise me, but I think

I'll turn the tables and fly up there this afternoon." He became brisk again. "Thanks, Ben and keep up the good work."

"Thank you sir." Ben waited until David severed the connection and then replaced the handset, relief flooding across his face. His concern about David Kendall's reaction when he found out about his broken leg had been unfounded. He should have known that would be the case—the man had always treated him fairly. He eased the bulky cast up onto a stool and sat back, thankful to have crossed that hurdle.

David Kendall made a few quick phone calls, glancing frequently down at his dock. His waterfront home at Deep Cove was ideal in that it offered quick access to the airport, the ferry terminal, and it had a dock for his float plane—his preferred method of transportation. His Cessna was prepped and ready to go.

Finished with his calls, he spoke briefly with his housekeeper and strode purposely down the stairs leading to the dock. He was quickly airborne, and as usual his troubles melted away. Gaining altitude, he looked down at the sparkling ocean, dotted with islands. The sight never failed to thrill him and he relaxed, the miles falling away behind him as he headed north to The Lodge. It would be good to sit quietly with Bill and get caught up on his friend's news.

Iridescence on the surface of the water caught his attention and he dropped down for a closer look. This far north, in the shipping lanes, there wasn't much small boat traffic. He ground his teeth angrily. It was almost impossible to catch tankers and other large boats when they flushed their bilges. The oil slick was almost dissipated and there were no vessels in the area, but he noted the position. Even without GPS it would have been easy to find again, just to the west of a string of small islands. He would report it when he arrived at The Lodge.

Gray dropped his end of the log.

"Hey!" said Erin "What are you . . ."

He held up a cautionary hand. "Do you hear that?" He tilted his head to the side and she found herself doing the same. "That's an aircraft engine."

Erin shielded her eyes, peering up at the sky. The breaking of the waves against the shore seemed to drown out every other sound, but she trusted Gray's instincts. "There!" she shouted, pointing just over the offshore islands. "Out there, above the islands."

"It's a float plane." Gray tried to hide his disappointment. "But I'm afraid it's too far out to see our sign." They had almost completed the last letter of their H-E-L-P sign.

Erin couldn't hide her disappointment. Her shoulders fell and she exhaled slowly, feeling as though her entire body was deflating. As a matter of fact, her jeans seemed to be riding a little lower on her hips. Between the limited diet and the extra physical work she'd been putting in, she supposed she might have lost a couple of pounds. The thought was appealing, but the truth was probably something more prosaic. The jeans must be stretching from constant wear. That was it.

She forced herself to put on a bright smile. "It would

have been better if they'd spotted us but even so I'm going to take it as a positive sign. Whoever it is will probably come back this way. Maybe he'll fly closer to land next time."

Gray smiled indulgently. "Yeah, it's a possibility. Come on, let's finish this 'P'."

"Did you see the float plane?" Erin joined Bill and Angela by the fire and reached for a cup of tea. There was always a can of hot water beside the fire. It was sobering how the gifts that had seemed frivolous and silly a week ago had become treasured possessions.

"Sure did." Bill waved his binoculars. "You'll never guess who it was!"

"You know?" Erin looked at him, disbelief on her face.

"I saw the call sign. It was David Kendall."

Footsteps muffled by the sand, Gray had come up behind her. "Who?"

"David Kendall." Bill was looking very pleased with himself. "Guess he was heading up to The Lodge."

"Huh." Gray seemed to be digesting this information.

"He was flying fairly low. I got the impression that he was looking at something on the water. He regained altitude once he was past the islands." Bill looked at Gray thoughtfully. "If there was any debris on the water it wouldn't still be around, would it?"

"I don't think so." Gray spoke slowly. "But there could still be a film of oil on the water. Most of it would have burned off in the explosion, but there's always the possibility." He looked around at the others. "But I wouldn't want to count on it too much. Especially since he kept on going."

Angela had remained focused on the spot where the aircraft had disappeared. "David Kendall. He's the man who owns The Lodge, isn't he?" She didn't wait for a response, but turned to the others, her eyes glowing. "We're as good as rescued. He'll talk to people at The Lodge, they'll realize we're overdue and he'll come back to look for us, I just know it."

David Kendall waved off the attentive waiter. "No thanks, Vince. One's my limit." He drained the last of the scotch and excused himself from the table. He usually enjoyed sitting with the guests, listening to their impressions of The Lodge, but tonight was different. Every few seconds his gaze had shifted beyond the plate glass windows. *Legend* should have arrived by now. He went through a door marked PRIVATE and took the stairs two at a time, exiting on the roof of the building. From this vantage point he could see far down the inlet, but tonight there was nothing to see except the golden glow of the setting sun.

Alarm bells started to sound in the back of his mind as he watched the sun sink into the sea. He couldn't have pointed to any one thing—it was more a general sense of unease. But over the years he'd learned to trust his instincts, and they had saved him more than once.

Ben answered after several rings. "Skookum Charters."

"Ben. I'm surprised you're still there. It's David Kendall here."

"Hello, Mr. Kendall. What can I do for you?"

"I'm at The Lodge now, and *Legend* hasn't arrived yet. Could I take you up on that offer to call them on the radio?"

Ben was silent for a moment. "Certainly sir. Would you like to stand by? I'll try them now."

David knew he was being foolish, but he had to satisfy that niggling feeling in the back of his mind. He listened as Ben picked up the radio.

"*Legend*, Skookum base. Come in please." The silence stretched out and he heard Ben clear his throat. "*Legend*, Skookum. Come in please."

Ben picked up the handset. "Sorry sir, he isn't replying, but I think I know why. I got a new inflatable this week and they've probably gone on shore to take advantage of the nice weather. You know, build a fire, have dinner. Maybe wander around a bit."

David thought he could hear the first hint of uncertainty in the young man's voice, but it was a reasonable explanation.

Ben went on. "I'll keep trying and call you back. Is ten o'clock too late? I don't think they'd stay on shore much later than that."

David checked his watch. It was 7:00. Ten seemed like forever. "Call me anytime. And thanks, Ben."

He grabbed the phone when it finally rang at ten minutes after ten. "Ben, is that you?"

"Yes, sir. I can't raise them." Ben swallowed audibly. "There's something I haven't told you, sir. Gray is on the boat. He insisted on being the first one to do a trip to The Lodge and he asked me not to mention it to anyone but . . ." his voice trailed off, then gained strength. "Do you think I should call the Coast Guard?"

David's thoughts swirled. "No, not yet. Could be their radio is out."

"Shouldn't be, sir. I had the entire system serviced last week. Had a short in the system."

"Let's not panic just yet. Gray is an excellent navigator. Besides, the Coast Guard can't go out tonight, and I've already decided I'm going to fly back along the coast as soon as it's light. What's that at this time of year? Five thirty?"

"Five-fifteen, sir."

"Well, there you go. I'll be ready for takeoff at first light. Give me a frequency where I can contact you."

David knew he wouldn't be able to sleep. He forced himself to eat a few mouthfuls of the delicious meal the kitchen had sent up then sat in front of the windows, coffee cup in hand. Why had he allowed his relationship with Gray to fall apart? It was the greatest regret of his lifetime and yet he didn't know how to put things right. He gave his head a brisk shake. This was no time to start dredging up old memories, old hurts. His focus now needed to be on finding Ben's boat. He intentionally hadn't told Ben about the oil slick. His first instincts about the slick being from a large boat were probably right and the young man had enough to worry about.

At four-thirty, he had a hot shower and shaved. He needed to be sharp this morning. As he left the resort, the sky was turning a pale grey, and the trees on the other side of the inlet were starting to become distinct. On his instructions, the Cessna had been topped up with gas.

Stepping onto the floats, he pushed off from the dock, relieved to be doing something concrete. He taxied away, sparing the guests the full effect of the engines, then pulled back on the controls and lifted off into the cool morning air.

The boat had probably anchored overnight in one of the myriad coves or inlets along the shore of the mainland. One thing was certain—they would head for a sheltered position. Perhaps the leeward side of an island.

The sun broke over the Coast Mountains in a blaze of glory, changing the landscape to one of contrasting light and shadow. Trees covered the mainland as far as he could see, broken only by irregular patches of logging. On the islands, trees clung precariously to the land, casting long shadows into the surrounding water. David slipped on his sunglasses and dropped down until he was only five hundred feet above the tops of the trees. Close enough to pick up any sign of people and yet high enough to see ahead. Out in the deep water a freighter was disappearing over the horizon. Another load of lumber bound for the insatiable Asian market.

Looking ahead, he spotted the string of islands where he'd seen the oil slick yesterday. He turned inland, so that he could approach it with the sun at his back. Focused on flying between the two largest islands, the H-E-L-P sign didn't register at first. The sun hadn't reached the beach yet, but the logs, bleached white from long exposure to the elements, contrasted with the sand. "Yes!" he shouted, pumping a fist in the air. Then, as quickly as it had come, his euphoria faded. There was no boat anywhere in sight. The sign had probably been made by some youngsters, thinking to pull a prank. But it was worth a second look. He flew out over deep water and turned around, noting that the oil slick had almost completely dissipated.

He came in from the south this time, flying parallel to the beach. What was that gray item, pulled up above high water? As he tried to place it, two figures emerged from behind a massive log, arms waving in the air. He was past them before he could wave, but he waggled his wings and headed out over the ocean again, weak with relief. The man was Gray, and the woman was his new chef, Erin.

He set the aircraft down with consummate skill and taxied toward the beach. Bill and a blond woman had joined Gray and Erin and everyone except Gray was grinning widely. Gray made a sign indicating that he could come close to the shore, then gave the cut-off sign and David killed the engine, floating closer to the shore until the floats kissed the sandy bottom. He removed his headset, grabbed a line and a stake and hopped down onto the float and then into the water. It was up to his knees but he didn't notice. He held the tie-down rope in one hand, a tentative smile on his face as he strode through the water in Gray's direction. "Boy, am I glad to see you." He glanced around, including the others. "Where's the boat?" Gray relieved him of the rope and started fashioning a holdfast, revealing nothing of his emotions.

"David, you old rogue." Sensing the awkward moment, Bill stuck out his hand. "You're just in time for breakfast. We'll tell you all about it."

Erin smiled at the obvious affection between the two

men. They clapped each other on the shoulder, laughing and talking, avoiding the near disaster than had brought them together on this remote stretch of beach. Then, remembering his manners, David turned to Angela.

"Sorry about that, but Bill and I are old friends. And you are?" he asked, still smiling.

"Angela Siebring." She offered her hand.

"Any relation to Daniel Siebring?" She nodded, and he continued. "I had a drink with him last night."

Angela's eyes glowed at the mention of her husband's name. "Thank you for finding us," she said quietly, then stepped back.

"Erin." David offered his hand again. "I didn't know you were joining us so soon. It's because of you I'm here."

"Really?" She imagined all sorts of disasters. "Is anything wrong?"

"Not at all. Our current chef wanted to contact you, that's all. He can explain later."

He turned to Gray, who had just finished securing the boat. Gray looked up at him, and Erin sensed an odd undercurrent pass between the two men. David stepped forward. "Hello, son," he said and held out his hand.

For a moment Erin thought she hadn't heard correctly. Had David Kendall just called Gray 'son'? It was obviously a personal moment, but she couldn't tear her eyes away from the two men. Gray hesitated, and for a moment she thought he was going to refuse his father's hand. Then a mask seemed to slip in place, and he came forward, hand outstretched. "Hello, sir."

David made a move as if to hug his son, but Gray

cradled his arm. The sling was grubby and starting to fray. "You're injured," David said, frowning.

"It's nothing much." Gray looked down at the arm as though it belonged to someone else. "Just a dislocated shoulder." He raised his eyes and looked at Erin. "Your new chef helped me put it back in place." His eyes were cold and emotionless, and Erin found herself hoping that it was David who'd caused the sudden change, not her. Then guilt overwhelmed her. How could she wish such a thing? But antagonism radiated from Gray like heat from their fire, and she wondered if she'd ever learn the true story.

If David was disappointed at the reception from his son, he didn't show it in front of the group. "What happened to the boat?" he asked, addressing his comments to no one in particular. He looked up and down the beach as though the missing craft might appear. Then his face clouded over. "I saw an oil slick yesterday. Was that . . . did the boat . . . ?"

Bill nodded. "There was an electrical fire. Gray managed to get us off moments before it exploded." His voice cracked. "We owe him our lives."

"Good Lord." David spoke in hushed tones. "Then that's why . . ." He looked at Gray and gestured toward his own eyebrows.

Gray looked down at his feet. "Uncle Bill's making it sound like a bigger deal that it was."

Bill stepped forward. "Don't listen to him, David. We wouldn't be here if it weren't for Gray. And that's the truth."

Gray walked toward their shelter and David looked longingly at his son's retreating back. Erin could tell that he wasn't going to pursue the subject. He rubbed his hands briskly. "Now, we can either have a cup of tea here, or I can fly us all back to The Lodge for breakfast. What do you say?"

"I vote for The Lodge." Angela wasted no time in letting her wishes be known. "I've been away from Danny for too long."

"I'll go along with that." Erin looked at the Cessna. "Will we all fit inside?"

"Absolutely." David jerked his head toward the sign. "But before we go, Bill and I will move a few of those logs around. It would be a pity if someone else landed here for nothing."

"Right. It'll only take a couple of minutes to gather up our stuff and douse the fire. Be right back." Erin and Angela trudged across the sand. Ahead of them, Gray was already pouring their precious water supply on the fire.

"I knew he'd come back." Angela smiled serenely and slipped her arm through Erin's. "Come on, girlfriend, we have places to go."

The shake roof of The Lodge glowed in the early morning sunlight. Designed by a gifted architect, it appeared to belong in this remote setting, its natural woods and soft green stain blending with the surroundings.

"It's huge," she observed, counting the floors. "And look at all those windows."

David taxied to the dock and shut off the engines.

"Our guests never tire of looking at the view—even when it rains." He raised an eyebrow. "If you look closely at our website and our brochure you'll even see a picture of some of our guests fishing in the rain. Although I admit, it's a very small picture."

"If they're like Daniel, they'll fish in any weather." Angela looked up at the expanse of windows. "Does anyone know we're coming?"

"No." David hung up his headset and opened the door. "Ben tried raising you on the radio until ten o'clock last night. He thought you might have taken the inflatable and gone ashore. By then the guests had gone to their rooms." He paused. "But I wouldn't have told them in any event."

"I need to call Ben." Gray spoke for the first time since they'd climbed into the Cessna.

"Go ahead and use my office. He'll be standing by." Gray disappeared down a short hall and David turned to the other three. "Now, let's get you settled. Angela, I'll find your husband's room number. Bill, I arranged a room for you when I found out you were arriving on the boat, and Einar has already moved out of his suite so it's free for Erin. The restaurant is open for breakfast now, so as soon as you're settled, come back down and get something to eat."

Erin's suite was far more luxurious that she'd anticipated. A small, well-equipped kitchen occupied one corner and she shook her head, recalling the coffee cans, seaweed and the old chunk of metal that had served as her last culinary tools. An overstuffed chair beside the window was cleverly designed to swivel. She could curl up to read, watch satellite television, or gaze at the magnificent scenery.

But none of those options interested her and she headed for the bathroom, tossing her duffel bag on the bed as she passed through the bedroom. Stepping into the large shower, she groaned with pleasure and turned her face up to the hot water. Never again would she take for granted the luxury of a shower. After shampooing, she massaged conditioner into her scalp, smiling to herself as the tangled tresses parted effortlessly. Was it only yesterday that she'd sat on the sand beside Gray, confiding in him about wanting a shower? The boat trip already seemed like something that had happened in the distant past. And the time on the beach . . . looking back now, it had been fun. She had grown closer to her travelling companions, revealing more of herself than she'd done with anyone else. *Ever.* She turned around, letting the water beat on her back. And then there was Gray. Learning that David Kendall was his father had shocked her in more ways than one. She rinsed her hair automatically, wondering how this new twist would affect their interaction. He knew she'd find out eventually, so why had he kept it a secret? And why was there such animosity between father and son? She turned off the tap. No, that wasn't quite right. The animosity wasn't between them, it was all one-sided.

She hadn't been mistaken this morning. That had been love and pride on David Kendall's face when he looked at his son. So why wasn't the affection returned? She lifted a large, fluffy towel from the heated rack and dried briskly, reminding herself that she was David's employee. What went on between him and his son was none of her business. She looked at herself in the mirror and smiled. If Gray wanted to confide in her, that was a different story.

Going back into the bedroom, she noticed her two large suitcases in the closet. She'd sent them a couple of weeks ago and promptly forgotten about them. Her eyes returned to the duffel bag. It held a change of underwear and a clean pair of off-white slacks and a black jersey top. Tying her hair back with an emerald green scarf she examined herself in the mirror. Her eyes sparkled back at her and she turned back to the duffel bag, rummaging around for the small bag that contained her meager supply of jewelry. What had Trudy said when she gave her those hoops? Something about elongating her face? She put them on and jiggled her head, unaccustomed to the way they bounced against her neck. But they looked good, and she left them on and headed downstairs to the restaurant.

Chapter Eight

Erin stopped at the entrance to the restaurant. Where was everyone? She glanced at her watch. Of course, it was still early. David's whirlwind rescue had taken place before many of the guests were even awake. Except for those early birds who'd already gone fishing. She'd become attuned to the rhythm of the place soon enough.

Bill and David were at a window table, engrossed in conversation. She didn't feel like sitting with them and was pondering how to excuse herself when she sensed a presence behind her.

"Erin, is that you?" Gray's voice purred in her ear. She turned around and almost bumped into him. His hair was damp from the shower and he wore a pale blue denim shirt, the sleeves rolled up. As on that first morning at the dock, she caught a whiff of his aftershave, and her knees weakened.

She tossed back her hair, struggling to appear cool but getting the distinct impression that he wasn't buying her act. "Gray," she said breathlessly. Even with his eyebrows mostly gone his appeal was almost visceral. He was so close she could see that his eyelashes were already lengthening. When they grew back completely, heaven help her!

"I see you got your shower." His voice was a lazy drawl. "And now how about some breakfast?"

She nodded, not willing to trust her voice. He placed his hand at the small of her back and guided her across the room to a table tucked in a comer. Bill and David acknowledged them as they passed, then returned to their conversation.

He held out her chair and she sat down gratefully. A waiter appeared like magic, setting down two glasses of orange juice, two glasses of iced water and a carafe of coffee.

"It's regular," he said cheerfully, placing two delicate cups and saucers before them, "but I can bring some decaf if you wish." He turned his attention to Erin. "Welcome to The Lodge, Miss Delaney. And welcome back, Mr. Kendall."

"Thanks, Brendan. I think we both prefer the regular this morning." He queried Erin with a slight raise of what used to be his eyebrows and she nodded her agreement.

The waiter poured coffee and disappeared.

"I see you've ditched your sling." Erin held the porcelain cup with two hands, inhaling the fragrance.

Gray rotated his shoulder. "Yeah. It's still a bit sore,

but it feels much better after a hot shower." He took a deep swallow of coffee, dark blue eyes looking at her steadily. "You look different somehow."

She lifted the cup, savoring the rich smell. "I feel different," she said, groping for words. "You know, I think it's just now starting to sink in." Her emotions caught up with her and her hands began to tremble. She set down her cup. "We came very close to being killed out there, but we were all too busy for it to register. That's probably a good thing, when you think about it."

"But we survived." He laid his hand over hers. "Thanks mostly to you."

Her head came up sharply. "You're not going to start that again, are you? We all did our part. That's what's so great." She looked down at his hand. It was large and competent, and it awakened a deep, visceral longing that had been building ever since that very first morning when she saw him on the deck of the boat. A need to be held, to be cherished, to belong to this man, to be taken care of by him.

The idea was so preposterous that she shook her head, trying to clear it of such nonsense. He sensed the change in her and pulled back slowly, studying her with cool detachment. "You know something, Erin? You're probably the most complex woman I've ever known."

"And I suppose you've known plenty." The words were out before she could stop them.

The lazy smile was back. "I've known my share."

She had to know. "And how about now? Tell me about the woman in your life right now."

Something dark surfaced behind his eyes then slid away. But the light was gone from them and she regretted giving voice to her curiosity.

"Right now?" He reached below the table and massaged his thigh, a reflexive gesture. "There was someone, but she didn't have any use for damaged goods. You see, she loved to party, loved to dance, and I'm not much good in that department anymore."

"The stupid woman." Erin's anger flared. "You're probably better off anyway. Why, nobody in their right mind would . . ." She clamped her jaw shut.

"Would what, Erin?" He leaned forward and she found herself being pulled into those mesmerizing eyes. How could any woman resist him? All rational thought fled from her mind, and she reached for her coffee cup, playing for time.

"Erin!" A tall, white-jacketed figure moved through the tables. He was strikingly handsome, with blond hair and pale blue eyes.

Erin forced a smile onto her face and stuck out her hand. "Hello, Chef." He wore the familiar knotted napkin around his neck. Until she officially took over, he would be referred to as 'Chef' in this establishment. "Do you have time for a coffee?" She was fairly confident that he would say no.

"Thank you, but no." He turned to Gray and laid a friendly hand on his shoulder. "I hear you had a bit of an adventure on the way up."

"You could say that." Gray nodded. "But we made it."

"Yes, yes. That's good then." If Erin listened carefully, she could hear a faint German accent. He turned back to her. "Could you stop by the kitchen later? I have a few things to ask you."

"Certainly." She glanced at Gray. "We were just about to order some breakfast."

"Good. I'll see you later then." He wandered over to greet David and Bill.

"Cheerful chap." Erin picked up the carafe and poured more coffee in Gray's cup, then her own.

He sat patiently while she poured a dollop of cream in her cup. "Now," he said when she was finally settled. "Where were we?"

She opened her mouth to give him a flippant answer then thought better of it. Her theories of yesterday didn't hold water any more. He didn't need her on his side to retain the contracts to fly guests to The Lodge. He was David Kendall's son, for goodness sake! So why was he sitting here, with her? The thought raised a rash of goosebumps along her forearms. She could brush him off with a clever remark, or she could find out where she stood.

"We were talking about your girlfriend. The dancer."

"Oh, that! That was over long ago, but it still rankles." He raised his eyes. "No, what I meant is where are *we*?" He hunched over the table. "You and me. Where are we going here?"

They were the words she'd longed to hear. For a moment she wondered if she'd imagined them, but one look at his face told her that she wasn't dreaming. A warm feeling of belonging came over her. "I'm not sure, Gray but I'd like to find out." Emboldened by her own words, she squared her shoulders and looked directly at him. "When you're ready to find out, you'll know where to find me."

This time his smile lit up his eyes. "That's what I wanted to hear." He ran a finger along the back of her hand. "I wish I didn't have to go back so quickly, but a buddy is coming for me this morning. I spoke with Ben and there's a ton of paperwork to be done to get his claim going."

"Oh my gosh, I'd forgotten about that." She stilled, her coffee cup halfway to her lips. "Was he shattered about losing the boat?"

"He took it fairly well, actually. Mainly he was concerned about us. He's already talking about getting a bigger boat."

"So you're leaving?" *Why did it have to happen this way?* She glanced around the restaurant. Most of the tables were now filled, but she hadn't noticed the guests coming in.

He glanced at his watch. "In about forty-five minutes." The waiter arrived and Gray ordered steak and eggs. "I might as well eat a good meal while I can. I have a feeling I'm going to have a busy few days coming up."

"Me, too." Erin lowered her voice. "When Chef stopped by earlier I sensed an impatience to get going. I think he's going to ask me to take over now that I'm here." She shrugged. "Just a feeling."

"Don't let him pressure you if you need time." He was suddenly businesslike and Erin knew he'd be surprised if he could see how closely he resembled his father at that moment. "I'm sure his contract with The Lodge is tight."

"No doubt." Erin nodded to herself. "But if he asks, I think I'll agree." She gave him a slow smile. "It'll make the time pass more quickly."

They chatted comfortably throughout the meal. Erin asked him about operating a charter air business, and he asked some very astute questions about running a kitchen. Their plates had scarcely been cleared away when a seaplane made a perfect landing and taxied toward the dock.

"There's my ride." Gray stood up and held her chair. "Walk out with me?"

She nodded and preceded him out of the restaurant. In the area that served as reception and lounge a fire crackled in a massive fieldstone fireplace.

"I know what you're thinking," he whispered into her ear. "You're thinking that our fire back on the beach was every bit as good."

"It *was* good, wasn't it?" She wanted to reach out, to hold him back. There were so many things to learn about him and now he was leaving. But she couldn't bring herself to ask him when she'd see him again. With a backward glance at the fire she followed him out onto a broad deck. Steps led down to the dock below and she hesitated, unsure of how far he wanted her to accompany him. Besides, down there everyone in the restaurant could see them.

Taking her hand, he guided her off to the side where they were sheltered from inquisitive eyes. Still holding her hand, he raised it to his lips. It was becoming a familiar gesture, and she knew that she'd never get enough of it. "So you're going to be all right?" His lips moved against her hand and she felt heat rising up through her body. She could think of a much better place for those lips.

"Uh-huh." Such a brilliant response! Where were her clever words now that she needed them? A breeze caught her hair, tugging it free from its restraints, swirling it around her face. He brushed it away tenderly, raking his fingers through the lustrous strands. Out here in the brilliant sun his pupils had shrunk to pinpoints, the blue of his eyes matching the deep water of the inlet. She swayed toward him and he pulled her closer, freeing his fingers from her hair and sliding them around her neck, pulling her face forward.

"I'm going to miss you, Erin Delaney." His lips brushed lightly over hers and he pulled back, watching her with an intensity that took her breath away. She leaned forward and his arms came around her, cradling her with a gentleness that threatened to buckle her knees. He nibbled at her mouth, and she opened her eyes to see him smiling at her. Then he deepened the kiss and she held on, reveling in the myriad of sensations that raced through her body.

"Wow," he said, his voice a deep, husky growl. "We'd better stop this before I throw my responsibilities out the window."

"Can't have that," she said, wishing just the opposite.

He released her with obvious reluctance and she followed him to the railing of the deck. "I'll call you," he said at the top of the stairs and she nodded mutely.

He ran down the ramp and greeted his friend. Before she knew it, they were gone, lifting off from the sun-flecked surface of the inlet, water streaming away behind the floats. She stood on her tiptoes, watching the aircraft until it banked and disappeared. For several minutes she remained at the railing, trying to recapture the thrill of his lips against hers. But she couldn't. Like everything else these past few days, it seemed unreal. She turned and walked back into the great room.

She walked into the kitchen, nodding to several employees along the way. The chef was in his office and stood up as she entered, removing a gift box of smoked salmon from the one chair beside his desk. "A sample from one of the suppliers," he said. "They don't seem to understand that our guests prefer fresh salmon. Especially if they've caught it themselves." He held out the box, offering it to her.

"No thanks," she said. "Smoked salmon isn't my favorite thing. But wherever you're going, it will make a great gift."

"That's what I thought." He tossed it on a credenza behind him. Erin tried not to stare at the cluttered office. He probably knew where everything was, and that's what counted.

"You'll like it here," he said with no preamble. "It's a good place to work. Connor Fairbairn is an excellent manager and David insists that everything be top quality. I like that." He searched for something on his desk and finally unearthed a printout. "But we've had a problem with our produce. We need to change suppliers, and I thought you should choose." He grinned. "That way, if the next batch isn't fresh you can blame yourself."

"Thanks a lot." She perused the list and pointed to her choice. "Do you want to make the call, or shall I?"

"I need to place an order today so I'll do it. But I'll make sure they know you're coming on board and that you chose them."

She smiled. "They'll probably remember me from the restaurant in Victoria. I've never had any problems with them."

"Excellent." He tossed the printout on his desk. "So. You came early, huh?"

Erin heard eagerness in his voice. Her instincts had been right, but she'd wait for him to ask her. "Yes. I thought it couldn't hurt to get to know the place."

"Good idea." He looked up as though he'd just come up with a brilliant idea. "But if you want to take over early, it's okay with me."

She laughed. Couldn't help it—he was so transparent. "You're anxious to get going, aren't you?"

He grinned. "Yeah."

"How about the day after tomorrow? That will leave tomorrow for you to show me around." She paused. "If it's okay with Connor, that is."

He managed a sheepish grin. "I already asked him. He says if you agree it's fine with him." He held out at hand. "Thanks, Erin."

David and Bill were standing in the lounge when she exited the kitchen and David beckoned her over. Physically they were opposites, Bill being short, dark and balding in contrast to David's height and silvery hair. But they were easy in each other's company, the mark of good friends. "I see you visited the kitchen." David leaned casually against one of the massive leather chairs that flanked the fireplace. "What did you think of it?" Once more she was struck by the resemblance between father and son, right down to the sprinkling of premature grey in Gray's hair.

"From what I saw it looks quite efficient." She hesitated then plunged forward. "Chef says he's cleared it with Connor to leave early. I told him I'd like a day with him tomorrow and that I'd be prepared to take over the next day."

"Great. I'll still be here then." Bill beamed his approval. "I'm getting used to your cooking."

"Sorry, we're fresh out of mussels."

David watched the interaction with interest. "There's one thing we can be sure of," he said with a grin. "You won't have to boil water in coffee cans and cook food wrapped in seaweed."

"It wasn't so bad," said Bill, exchanging a private smile with Erin. "I wouldn't have missed it for the world."

"Bill's been telling me what a rock you were." David seemed to be eyeing her with a new appreciation. "He says you were the glue that held everyone together."

Erin glared at the older man. It was becoming tiresome refuting everyone's exaggerated description of her efforts.

Bill looked at her affectionately. "She doesn't like to be fussed over, this one." He turned back to his friend. "But I can tell you from first hand experience, you've got a winner here."

"All right you two, this is getting embarrassing. I'm

outta here!" She touched Bill on the arm. "Don't forget to take your pills, and I'll see you later. Right now I'm going to unpack and get settled."

The transition was surprisingly easy. The condition of the chef's office notwithstanding, the kitchen ran smoothly and efficiently. Erin began to wonder if she'd made a mistake in coming here. Would there be enough of a challenge to hold her interest?

"Don't worry," said Yvonne, sensing her dismay. "When there's a full house you'll be wishing we all had four arms." She tossed some left-over onion into a stockpot and adjusted the flame. "It can get hectic in here." She shook her head. "When the men come in from a day of fishing, they're famished."

"What about the women? What do they do while the men are fishing?"

"Quite a few actually go out. But the ones who don't fish seem to keep themselves busy. The Lodge offers eco tours up the inlet, and they go whale watching in season, but I think they really come for the spa."

"I saw the doorway leading to the spa." Erin turned over a loaf of bread fresh from the oven, tapped the bottom and replaced it on the cooling rack. "Very elegant. Frosted glass, a jungle of plants, muted lights and soft music." She felt suddenly out of her depth. "You know, I've never been to a spa."

"Never?"

"Never. I don't know why." She hesitated. "Actually, I do. I always thought a day at the spa was for other people, but not for me."

"But it's free for you!" Color flooded Yvonne's cheeks and she clapped a hand over her mouth. "Sorry, Chef. It's none of my business, but I've heard that all of the management people get free spa services."

Erin thought back to the terms of her contract. Yvonne was right, complimentary spa services had been part of the package, but at the time she'd dismissed the idea, focusing instead on the items that interested her. She caught sight of her distorted reflection on the door of one of the stainless steel refrigerators. Now that she was starting to feel more positive about herself, the idea of a day of pampering was very appealing. She nodded briskly at her reflection then gave the breakfast chef a broad grin. "Thanks for the reminder."

Erin threaded her way between the dining room tables, pausing to exchange pleasantries with a few of the guests. The Lodge catered to mostly wealthy guests. At least it seemed that way. Many were flown in on their own private aircraft, in spite of the service being offered by The Lodge. They expected excellent service, and they received just that. But unlike many of the regulars at the restaurant in Victoria, they were not loud and demanding. She suspected that David Kendall instructed his people to weed out the undesirables. It made for an enjoyable work environment.

"Erin!" Angela waved to her. Clothed in a soft yellow sweater and matching slacks, she looked even more beautiful than the woman who had boarded *Legend*. They had chatted a few days ago and Erin wasn't surprised to learn that Daniel had greeted Angela with open arms. And now, after almost a week at The Lodge, Angela glowed with happiness.

Angela motioned to the chair beside her. "Do you have time for coffee? Come sit down. You won't believe who's here!" She was bubbling over with excitement.

Erin's stomach did a little flip-flop and she looked outside, scanning the dock for a familiar aircraft, only to be disappointed again. Each day she didn't hear from Gray made her doubt what had passed between them. "Who?" She accepted half a cup of coffee from the hovering waiter and waved away a plate of fresh croissants.

"Magda!" Angela was almost bouncing in her seat. "Remember, I told you about her. She does eyebrows in Victoria, but she's come up here for a few days to work in the spa. Everybody's thrilled."

Erin tried to hide her disappointment. "That's great."

"I knew you'd say that and I've had the most wonderful idea. Let's go together. Eyebrows, manicure, and pedicure. My treat."

Erin set down her cup. "You don't have to do that." She glanced around at the other guests and lowered her voice. "I get those services for free."

"Nonsense. Magda will be booked the entire time she's here and besides I know you."

Erin couldn't help but laugh. "You do?"

"I do. You'd talk about going, but you'd never get around to it. But if I book it for you, then you have to show up." She nodded her head emphatically. "So you see, you're not the only one who can get things done."

"I didn't say—"

"Erin." Angela held up her hands in a gesture of surrender. "I was kidding. Lighten up."

Erin straightened the cutlery on the table. "Okay, confession time. I've never been to a spa. Will you help me through it?"

"What time can you make it?"

"Today?" This was all going rather fast.

Angela rolled her eyes. "Well yeah!"

"I don't know." Her presence wasn't required in the kitchen until later in the afternoon. "Almost anytime, I guess."

"Good, because our booking is in half an hour."

"You're impossible."

"Of course I am." Angela smiled sweetly and rose from the table. "I'll meet you there."

The spa experience had been surprisingly enjoyable and Erin wondered why she'd never done it before. In addition to brow shaping, manicure and pedicure, they'd indulged in hair styling. Erin couldn't remember feeling so pampered. As they were changing back into their clothes she turned to her friend. "You set up that part with that hairdresser, didn't you!" She tried to sound stern, but it didn't work.

Angela pulled back, admiring Erin's hair once more. "Actually, I didn't. Honest." She ran her hands through the newly feathered hair. "But when she stopped by our station and commented on your beautiful hair I wanted to hug her."

Erin studied her reflection in the mirror. "I hardly

recognize myself." Expertly cut and styled, her hair fell in soft curls around her face, framing her new eyebrows.

"I knew it could look like this." Angela eyed the results, lifting a strand of hair away from Erin's forehead with a quick, experienced hand. "It's gorgeous. And you were right to be firm about not wanting any color. If I had hair like yours, I'd leave it alone too." She looked down at Erin's feet. What was the name of that nail polish?"

"Baja Baby." Erin made a face. "Where do they come up with these names?"

"I don't know." Angela pulled Erin down into a chair, suddenly serious. "Are you happy here Erin? Your color's good, but you look a bit thinner." Her eyes darkened with concern.

Erin looked past her friend, catching another glimpse of herself in the mirror. "You really think so? No, I'm fine and the job is great." She took another peek in the mirror. "But I have noticed that all my slacks are a bit looser." Her thoughts drifted back over the last couple of weeks. "Do you remember that long hot spell we had about a month ago? Well, I started eating fruit and salads instead of my usual diet and I've kept it up since I came here." She patted her flat stomach. "It feels good, though . . . unfamiliar, but good."

"Just promise me you're not doing anything unhealthy. You know how I feel about unnatural weight loss."

"Yes, Mom. I promise." Erin saluted.

"That's all right then." Angela rose and the friends headed back toward the main lounge. "I almost hate to go home tomorrow. It's been like a second honeymoon." She reached inside her handbag and slipped a card from a small metal case. "Here's my business card in case I miss you tomorrow morning. Call me anytime you get back to the city, okay?"

"Okay." Erin gave the slender woman a hug, blinking back tears. "I'll do that."

Erin wound up her hair, tucking it beneath the chef's beanie. It startled her every time she looked in the mirror. Fortunately, that didn't happen too often. The wall phone outside her office buzzed and she lifted up the receiver. "Hello?"

"Erin." She sat down with a thud on the stairs leading up into her office. "Are you there?"

"Yes, I'm here." Her voice sounded strange. But it was surprising that she could hear it at all over the pounding in her ears. The kitchen staff was giving her odd looks.

"I'm glad I caught you. I just got in."

"Just a sec, okay?" She jumped up. "I'm going to put you on hold."

She closed the door to her office and picked up the phone. "That's better. Every eye in the kitchen was on me. It's such a small place, everybody seems to know everyone else's business." She laughed shakily, realizing that she was babbling. "How are you?"

"Hungry." His voice was low, husky and suggestive. Or was that her imagination running wild?

"Sorry. No trout on the menu today."

"I wasn't thinking of food." His voice caressed her.

"Oh." Heat suffused her body. She pulled off her

beanie and her hair tumbled around her shoulders. She'd waited for this call all week and now she couldn't think of a thing to say.

"Have you got a bathing suit?"

She thought of the simple one-piece black suit folded neatly in the corner of one of her drawers. It had been the most flattering one she could find. "Yeah, I guess so."

"Good. How about tomorrow?"

"Tomorrow?"

"Why are you repeating everything I say?"

She closed her eyes. *Why? Because I'm tongue-tied. Because I'm over the moon that you called and I'm already terrified that something is going to go wrong. Because I'm afraid I'll fall in love with you.*

She gave herself a mental slap. "You just took me by surprise, that's all." She called up tomorrow's schedule on the computer even though she already knew it. "Tomorrow looks good. What time?"

"That's more like it. I figure if I get there around eleven we can fly up to the hot pools, have a dip and then if I can impose on a certain chef I know, we could have a picnic. I could have you back in time for dinner."

"Sounds good. I think I can rustle us up something to eat."

"I'm counting on it." He paused. "And Erin?"

"Yes?"

"Nothing. I just like saying your name." He chuckled softly. "Bye."

Chapter Nine

Erin paced the floor of the deck, pausing every few moments to shade her eyes and look into the distance. The picnic basket and a small tote bag waited beside the ramp. Since talking to Gray yesterday, she'd had a difficult time concealing her excitement. She didn't care if she appeared eager to anyone who might be watching. She didn't want to waste a moment of the day.

"Waiting for someone?" Bill sauntered out onto the deck. He looked rested and content and she gave him an impulsive hug.

"I'm waiting for Gray. When we were stuck on that beach he promised to take me to a spot along the coast where there's a series of hot pools." She scanned the horizon. "Today's the day."

Bill lifted his binoculars. "I think I see him." He lifted the strap over his head and handed them to her. "Have a look." He moved behind her while she focused. "Line up with the right hand side of that island."

Erin gasped. "Wow. It's larger than I thought." She studied the approaching aircraft. "The wings are big, aren't they? They seem to go across in one piece. I don't think I've ever seen anything like it."

"That's not surprising. There aren't very many left in the world. Fortunately the ones that are left are well maintained. They're owned by people with pretty deep pockets."

"I hope Gray doesn't fit that description." She lowered the binoculars slowly.

"Why not?"

It was a fair question, but it was one that Erin wasn't sure she could answer. "I don't know, Bill. It's not like I've had trouble with rich men or anything, but I've seen plenty of them in my various jobs and money doesn't seem to make them any happier." The aircraft flew past and commenced a long, banking turn, its powerful motors shattering the silence of the morning. "I haven't known Gray for very long, but I get the impression that he could use a good dose of happiness."

Bill gave her an odd look. "You might be right."

Much like its namesake, the aircraft skimmed the water then settled down comfortably. Gray taxied up to the dock and was greeted by one of the maintenance men, who waited until the propellers stopped turning, then guided the long tapered wing over the dock. Gray offloaded several cartons of material, which were stacked on a dolly and whisked away by a second staff member.

Bill stuck out his hand. "Good-bye, Erin. My son

should be arriving any minute. We're having lunch here and then he's flying me back to Victoria."

Erin studied the familiar face. "I'm going to miss you, Bill Corbett. I've gotten used to seeing you around."

"Me too." His voice was husky. "But I have a feeling we'll be seeing each other again." He pulled her into a quick embrace then released her, pointing to the picnic basket and bag. "Better not keep that young man waiting."

Lost for words she nodded, then gave his arm a gentle squeeze before heading down the ramp. She hadn't expected to feel this way about her traveling partners, but when Angela had left this morning, she'd had to work hard to keep from crying.

"What is it?" Gray's concern was instant.

She smiled through the threatening tears. "It's nothing, really." She passed him the basket and dabbed at her eyes. "I said good-bye to Angela this morning, and now Bill tells me he's leaving this afternoon. I'm going to miss them, that's all. Just ignore me."

"Not a chance."

He leered at her and she gave him a good-natured swat. "Come on, let's get out of here."

He showed her where to place her foot and she entered the cabin. The interior was exquisite—comfortable upholstered seats complemented by glowing teak woodwork. Understated yet luxurious, it would impress even the most jaded traveler.

"It's lovely," she said, running a hand over the back of a chair and noting the Grumman logo stitched into the rich fabric. "How long have you had it?"

"Not long. I had it completely restored at a shop on the Victoria airport. Mike's become famous for his work on Mallards. There are less than thirty left operating in the world." He showed her up to the cockpit, got her settled in the co-pilot's seat and handed her a pair of headphones. "You'll need these. It's noisy."

"So we noticed when you flew by. Those are big motors."

"Engines." He nodded to the employee on the dock, who pushed them off. "Pratt & Whitneys." The engines roared into life and they began to move, water rushing past the hull with such force that it began to vibrate.

Erin looked at him nervously. "Is this normal?" she asked, teeth chattering.

He adjusted the mouthpiece on his headset. "Quite normal." He pulled back on the controls, easing them gently into the air. "You'll get used to it."

She pondered his remark as they gained altitude. She could get used to Gray Kendall very easily. Did she dare to dream of a future with this man? They leveled out and she looked down at the now familiar landscape. It appeared different from the last time she'd flown over it in David's aircraft. Or was it her perception that was different? Self-doubt was almost a thing of the past these days as her confidence increased. She'd even fussed over her appearance this morning, thinking as she did so that she couldn't remember the last time she'd applied eye shadow.

Gray flew with the same intensity she'd seen when he piloted the boat. Safe in his hands, she sat back and enjoyed the rest of the flight.

"There," she said, pointing through the windshield. "That must be it. I can see the steam."

They crested a ridge, and below them the pools spilled down to the sea. Tipping the aircraft up on one wing, Gray circled the area, giving her an eagle's eye view. "I'll land into the wind and taxi up to that little beach," he informed her through the headphones. "We'll have to scramble over the rocks to get to the pools, but it isn't far."

Erin examined the beach below. "Is it safe?"

"It's small, but perfectly safe. I've checked it out a couple of times with a boat, just to be sure. Looks like we have the place to ourselves today."

They settled on the second to last pool, the ones higher up being too hot. Erin had examined the pools with interest, pulling back at the noxious smell where the water boiled up from the depths of the earth.

"One good thing about these lower pools. You can't smell the sulfur down here." Gray tossed his T-shirt onto a rock, unbuckled his belt and pulled down his jeans, revealing a blue bathing suit. Erin tried not to stare. She'd always thought that a woman swooning over a man's body was ridiculous. But that was then.

Broad shoulders tapered down to a narrow waist and dark tufts of hair sprinkled his chest, narrowing down to a thin line and disappearing into the swim trunks. His legs were strong and muscular. The scar on his left leg wasn't visible and she wondered if he was consciously keeping it from her view. Tearing her eyes away, she pulled her top over her head and fumbled in her bag for the ornate comb she'd brought to hold up her hair. With a quick twist she piled her hair on top of her head and jammed the comb into it. The breeze cooled her neck and she shivered.

"Cold?" His eyes clouded with concern. "Come on, get out of your slacks and let's get in." He perched on the side of the pool and eased himself into the steaming water with an appreciative sigh.

Erin tugged off her slacks and slid into the water. It was the first time in years that she hadn't been self-conscious about her body.

"Oh my gosh," she said, leaning her head back against the rim of crusted minerals. "This is heaven."

"I thought you'd enjoy it."

They remained silent for several minutes. A seagull drifted overhead, riding the air currents.

"I wonder what he thinks when he looks down here and sees us?" She squinted up at the bird.

"I dunno. He probably thinks we're crazy." Gray rolled his head in a circular motion, rotating his shoulders.

"Tired?" she asked softly, imitating his motion.

"A little. I ferried a plane out to Manitoba for a friend and spent several days looking around at available aircraft, but after all that I've decided to buy one here on the island." He raised his head, looked at her. "I think I told you I wanted to purchase another one."

So that was why he hadn't called! She hoped the relief didn't show on her face. "So when did you get back?"

Dark blue eyes held hers. "Yesterday. A few minutes before I called you."

She sank farther down into the water. "Oh."

"I thought about you a lot while I was away."

"You did?"

He held her eyes. "Yes. I thought about the way I was so rude to you when you showed up at the dock that first morning. And how you rowed us to shore, and built the fire pit and the shelter almost single-handed." He paused to take a breath. "And then how you cooked for us."

That was old news. "Is that all?"

"No. I was sorry that I hadn't told you the great David Kendall's my father. It wasn't fair to let you go on about him."

"I wasn't going on!" The lack of anything personal in what he was saying was making her angry.

He flicked a drop of water in her direction. "And there's something else."

She raised an eyebrow.

"I missed you."

"Oh." Her anger dissolved. "I missed you too." There, she'd said it!

"Good." He edged closer and extended his hand, fingertips meeting hers. The touch was innocent and yet terribly intimate. They remained that way for several long moments, connected by their fingertips and the longing in their eyes. Then Gray gave her hand a squeeze and smiled self-consciously. "Had enough?" He rose from the pool.

Erin was caught off-guard. She'd never been in a relationship—even a short-term one—where a man had been so restrained. Instead of disappointing, his reaction made her quietly hopeful.

She watched the water stream from his body. His left

side was turned toward her and he didn't seem self-conscious about the scar on his leg. It had turned an angry red from the heat of the pool.

"So tell me," she said, deliberately focusing on the scar. "What's so bad about that?"

He picked up his towel and dried his torso and arms with a few deft movements. "Nothing, I suppose but then it depends on who's looking." He held out his hand and pulled her from the pool. For a moment they stood close together, steam rising between them. A slow smile slid across his face. "It doesn't hold me back from doing the important things in life."

She swallowed. "Like flying."

He handed her the other towel. "Among others."

His words hung in the air between them and she took the towel, aware of a flush of color creeping up her neck that didn't have anything to do with the hot pool. She dried her back and her arms then looped the towel around her neck before removing the comb and shaking out her hair. She was slowly becoming used to the way it fell around her head. Gray's eyes flared with appreciation but he didn't say anything. She smiled to herself as she followed him through the rocks and back to the beach.

"Seems like old times," he said, biting into a piece of chicken. "Eating out here on the beach." He opened the thermos and smelled the contents. "Coffee," he said, reaching for the mugs. "But I would have settled for tea."

"I know you like coffee." She said it quietly. "But I don't know much more than that."

He poured out two mugs of coffee and handed one to

her. "Fair enough. I promised to tell you and now seems as good a time as any." He finished the piece of chicken and deliberately wiped his fingers, marshalling his thoughts. Then his gaze swept out over the sparkling water and he seemed to be drifting back in time.

"When I was young we were a happy family. You can sense that when you're a kid, no matter what your parents think. But then when I was in high school, things changed almost overnight. My parents started to fight and the tension in our house was so thick you had to push your way through it. Dad yelling and Mom crying." He rubbed a hand over his face. "He was having an affair. Mom started drinking more and it got so bad I stopped bringing my friends home." He sent her a sheepish glance. "That might sound selfish of me, worrying about myself, but it's true. Sometimes I'd come home and hear them going at each other. I can still recall some of their conversations. All of a sudden words like 'infidelity' and 'affair' became part of my vocabulary. I got pretty good at creeping around the house listening to them. Once they were talking about counselling. It was my Dad's suggestion and she smacked him on the face so hard he left the room with a hand up to his cheek. That was when I knew that things would never get better."

He picked up a handful of pebbles and started tossing them into the water. "He stayed in the house until I was eighteen then they got a divorce and he left. I was barely civil to him when I saw him. For the first year or so he came to visit regularly but then the visits tapered off. He'd moved out to Deep Cove by then but I was only invited out there once." He tossed the remaining pebbles into the water. "I was particularly rude on that visit, I recall. Sometimes I'd see his picture in the paper attending functions with different women. It hurt so much that I finally stopped looking."

Erin raised her coffee to her lips. It had gone cold and she tossed it out. "And you still haven't forgiven him?"

"No. My mother never got her life back. He put her in a treatment facility a couple of times to dry out, but she always goes back to drinking. She moved to Florida to live with her sister and I think they have happy hour twenty-four seven. I saw her a few months ago and she's really aged."

"But the drinking isn't your father's fault, surely."

Gray gave her a sharp look. "That's one way of looking at it, but she started drinking right around the time they started having trouble. He obviously deserves some of the blame."

Erin decided to let the matter rest.

He leaned back on one elbow. "Know something? The first time I saw you I thought you were probably one of his women."

Stunned, she could only shake her head. "Gray how could you! I told you I was the chef."

He flushed. "Yeah, well I thought maybe he'd hired you to get next to you."

She gave him a wry smile. "I don't know whether to be flattered or insulted, but even so I can assure you that your father's not interested in me. Besides, he's twice my age."

"Fortunately for me, Bill came along and set me straight. Made me realize I'd been making an ass of myself."

"I won't disagree with you there." She poured some more hot coffee and sipped it thoughtfully. "Do you have any siblings?"

"No. I am an only child. Just as well, huh? I mean, why inflict that on more than one kid?"

"Oh, I don't know. It might have been nice to have someone to share it with."

"How about you? Do you have any brothers or sisters?"

Erin stared into her coffee mug. "One sister."

"You don't sound very enthusiastic. Don't you like her?"

Her head shot up. "Of course I do. I practically brought her up. Our mother died when Crystal was eleven and I was fourteen. And then four years ago Dad died. I promised him I'd take care of Crystal until she was twenty. And I did."

"I knew it!" He reached for a piece of carrot cake and took a large bite, looking at her speculatively. "I could tell that you're one of those people who've always looked after everyone else. Didn't I tell you that, back on the beach?"

"Yes you did." Erin pretended to follow the treetop flight of a bald eagle. She didn't want him to see the tears in her eyes.

"So what made you break free, to come up here?"

"It was time," she said finally. "For myself and for Crystal."

"Crystal. That's your sister's name?"

Erin nodded.

"What's she like?"

"She's beautiful. As a matter of fact, when Angela came tripping down the dock that morning, I thought Crystal had followed me."

His eyes narrowed. "Why would she do that?"

"Because I spoiled her. Because she wanted me to stay home and take care of her." Erin shrugged. "It's just the way she is."

"So that's why you were a bit frosty to Angela at first."

"Yeah. Silly, huh?"

"That couldn't have been easy, raising your sister." He watched her, waiting.

It felt good to share her concerns with someone else. "Sometimes I worry I didn't do a very good job. She's turned out to be completely self-centered. I'm not sure where I went wrong but I did my best. When I broke free to come here I knew I'd done the right thing."

"Seems to me you're giving yourself too much credit here."

She turned on him. "What does that mean?"

He held up a hand. "What I meant is that you're taking it all on yourself. You're assuming that it's your fault she turned out the way she did, which I doubt. Some people are takers and some are givers, and it's clear to me which one you are. So give yourself a break, huh?"

She nodded slowly. "I'd like to think you're right, but I know one thing for sure. It's time for her to stand on her own two feet." She turned to him. "Did your mom used to say that to you?"

"It was mostly my dad, but yeah."

They fell silent, lost in memories.

Gray glanced at his watch with a frown of annoyance. "I hate to say this, but I'd better get you back." They packed up in comfortable silence and trudged back to the Mallard.

The flight back was far too quick and Erin listened over the headset as Gray called ahead to The Lodge, informing them of his arrival. One of the staff was on the dock to meet them, steadying the aircraft as they unloaded the basket and stepped out onto the dock.

Gray walked her to the foot of the ramp. "Thanks for today," he said, setting down the basket. "I enjoyed it."

"Me too." She wanted to snuggle up to his broad chest, to be held by him again like the last time they'd parted. But she was aware of the guests in the lounge, watching their every move. "Thanks for sharing the pools."

"Any time." He picked up her hand and brought it to his lips. Suddenly she didn't care if everyone in the entire building was watching them. "I'm booked to come back this weekend with a party of three local guys. Maybe we can have coffee together, okay?"

"I'd like that."

He squeezed her hand then dropped it. "See you then."

He walked back to his aircraft, taking her heart with him.

Sunlight danced on the water of Victoria's inner harbour. Gray had arrived at the float plane dock early to perform an unnecessary check on the new Beaver. The aircraft balanced out his growing fleet nicely but the Mallard remained his favorite.

He looked out over the water. Flanked on two sides by the Parliament buildings and the Empress Hotel, the harbor was featured in many of the city's tourism promotions. This morning the small tugs that served as harbor taxis were doing their dance, spinning and bobbing around like gaily painted corks. He stopped to watch them as he'd done many times before.

"Hey!" A demanding shout startled him. "You with the charter company?"

Gray studied the man behind the voice, disliking him on sight. He was accompanied by two other men who had dropped their bags on the dock. He'd reluctantly turned down a two-day charter because these men had booked first and he was already wishing he'd handed them over to another charter firm. But he'd done enough of that already while he was helping Ben; he didn't want to get a reputation for being unreliable. He made a mental note to get serious about hiring another pilot.

"That's right." He walked forward with his hand outstretched, trying to appear welcoming. "You must be the party traveling to The Lodge."

"That's right." The man offered his hand for a perfunctory shake and the others followed suit.

Gray studied his passengers while loading their bags. These three men in their fifties symbolized everything he disliked about the so-called privileged class. They represented old Victoria—prestige, money and power. Their sons didn't serve in the military—or if they did, they didn't go to Afghanistan. With a sudden flash of insight he realized that except for their age they were nothing like his father. And for the first time in many years he felt a surge of pride for his father—pride that he was a self-made man who treated every one of his employees with respect.

The Beaver was equipped with headphones for each passenger. Gray had learned early on in his charter career that passengers were going to ask questions. It was much easier to communicate with them over the headphones than have them lean into the cockpit and shout in his ear. He'd checked them off on his list and found that the loud one who was now ensconced in the co-pilot's seat was Blaine Matthews, a familiar name in the local newspapers.

He turned his attention to the take-off. Victoria's inner harbour was becoming notoriously crowded and he wasn't able to relax until they were airborne and well away from the congested area.

They flew along the east coast of Vancouver Island and the passengers were silent, taking in the beauty laid out below. Gray was looking forward to crossing over to the mainland. In a couple of hours, he planned to fly over the site of the explosion and see if he could spot their shelter on the beach. It would be something to share with Erin while they had coffee together.

"So, how's the fishing at The Lodge? I hear they've been taking some big Chinook this year." Matthew's voice boomed in his earphones and Gray adjusted the volume downward.

"From all reports the fishing's been excellent this season." He tapped a small barometer with his finger. "And it looks like the nice weather is going to hold."

"What do you mean 'from all reports'? I should think Kendall's operation would provide information that's a bit more sophisticated than that." Matthews turned in his seat. "Don't you agree, boys?"

The other men muttered their agreement and Gray slammed his jaw shut and started to grind his back teeth. He hadn't done that since flying in Afghanistan. He forced himself to relax and to respond. "I'm an independent charter service, sir. I'm not directly connected with The Lodge."

"Is that so? I would have thought Kendall would run his own charter service. He's into everything else."

Gray managed not to betray any emotion at the mention of his father's name. "I wouldn't know, sir. I just know that it's a good contract to have." It felt odd defending his father, but it was the truth. His father may be many things, but he was fair in business.

"Is he up there much? At The Lodge?"

"Not really. Connor Fairbairn is the Operations Manager. I co-ordinate with him."

The man waved Gray's remarks away with the brush of a hand. "Yes, yes. I know that. I was just wondering if we'd run into the man himself." He looked back at his companions. "Remember the old days fellows? Remember how Kendall couldn't keep control of his wife?"

Gray was sure he hadn't heard properly. These men couldn't be talking about his mother! A nasty chuckle came through the headphones and he tensed. Part of him wanted to rip off the headphones to shut out the man's hateful words but he couldn't. He had to hear the rest.

"What was her name again? Judith, wasn't it?"

Through his growing rage Gray heard a mutter of agreement. "Yes, the lovely Judith was quite the girl back then. Spread her favors around quite liberally as I recall. Kendall should have divorced her when he caught her with the pro from the golf course. Don't know how he managed to hold his head up after that." His tone hardened. "We all thought he'd go soft after that, but we were wrong. Still kept his edge in his business dealings. If anything, he became more ruthless."

"I guess he had something to prove." One of the men in the back spoke up. Gray wanted to jump out of his seat the punch him in the face. Better still, he'd like to boot them all out right now—without a single parachute between them. He gripped the controls so hard his knuckles turned white. He couldn't remember ever being this angry. Blood pounded in his temples, a sign he recognized as rising blood pressure. He took several deep breaths, forcing himself to calm down. Thankfully, the passengers had fallen silent or else he might not have been responsible for what he said.

Concentrate he told himself grimly, scanning the instrument panel. *Concentrate.* He removed his sunglasses and rubbed his eyes, then slipped them back on.

Years of flying experience kicked in and he managed to gain control of himself. He shot a quick look at the man in the passenger seat and was surprised to see that Matthews had fallen asleep, head lolling against the side door.

Gray turned his attention back to the business of flying, but it was as if he had switched himself to automatic pilot. He was scarcely aware of making course corrections or of passing familiar checkpoints. His thoughts were back in his parents' home and he was crouched at the top of the stairs, listening to their angry voices.

"So what?" his mother was saying. "You never loved me. If you did, you'd spend more time with me. And now everybody's laughing at me." There had been the familiar clink of the Waterford crystal decanter against a glass. Odd that he should remember that decanter now. He hadn't thought about it for years, but he'd always checked it when he came home from school. He'd become expert at judging how intoxicated his mother would be by the level of the amber liquid.

He was back at the top of the stairs again, listening to his father's voice, soothing at first and then rising in frustration. That had always been the pattern—low, intense words followed by angry shouts and a slammed door. But it was his mother who'd stayed in the house while his father left. In his young mind he'd always imagined his father going to another woman. Distressed at first by his father's absences he'd become confused. Eventually the confusion had turned to hurt, then hardened into loathing. His mother had cajoled and flattered him, calling him the man of the house and he'd swelled up with pride, confident that he could protect her.

But he couldn't protect her from her addiction. It had taken him years to accept that fact and in those years he'd burned with hatred for the father who had cheated on his mother.

Or so it had seemed at the time. It had never occurred to him that his mother was the one being unfaithful. Why had he assumed it was his father who was at fault, when all along it had been the other way around?

He searched his memory. He'd been a day student at a private boy's school. He'd listened carefully while the boys talked about their parents' divorces, exchanging stories about how easy it was to play one parent off against the other. He recalled one day where the boys had spoken in hushed tones, discussing the reasons for their parents' divorces. In most cases it was determined that the fathers had 'fooled around', the mothers being held up as blameless victims. That had taken place in happier times—before he too had been scarred by parental separation.

The man in the passenger seat snorted and woke himself up, looking around the cockpit in confusion. "Where are we?" he asked groggily.

"Almost there." Gray knew his tone was abrupt, but it was the best he could manage under the circumstances. He pressed forward on the controls and they started to descend, leveling off at the mouth of the inlet. The guests always enjoyed seeing the area where they would be fishing. At this point he generally did a fly-by on a dramatic waterfall but today he flew straight ahead, foregoing his usual narrative. He landed hard and fast in front of The Lodge, taxiing up to the dock where he cut his engines and jumped out without a word.

"Hi, Gray." The young college student who served as baggage porter greeted him warmly. Gray nodded and opened the baggage hold, carelessly tossing the baggage onto the dock.

"Hold on there!" One of the men confronted him, bristling with annoyance.

Gray slammed the door of the hold, checking to make sure it was closed then brushed past him, stepping onto the float and climbing up into the pilot's seat. He looked back at the lodge employee. "Give me a shove, would you, Karl?" Eyes darting from the new arrivals to Gray, the man complied and Gray was gone. The entire procedure had taken less than five minutes.

Erin had been waiting for this day all week. She'd checked with Connor yesterday to find out when the new arrivals were expected, informing him that she'd be absent from the kitchen for an hour or two. This morning she'd appeared in the kitchen earlier than usual, raising a few eyebrows among the staff. It was impossible to keep a secret here, and the word had spread quickly about the boss's son and the new chef. Their adventure together on the supply boat and the subsequent rescue by David Kendall had kept tongues wagging for days. Between her exploits on the beach and her confident leadership in the kitchen, it hadn't taken her long to earn their respect. And now Gray Kendall was arriving and their new boss would be absent from the kitchen at the same time. Things were getting interesting.

Standing up on the deck, Erin heard the motors before she saw the aircraft. She knew it wasn't the

Mallard—there was no mistaking those powerful engines. The Beaver touched down right out in front, and her heart leaped when she recognized Gray in the cockpit, sunglasses reflecting the glare off the water. He taxied up to the dock and she raised her hand to wave then changed her mind. She'd greet him later when she could look into his eyes and see if anything had changed.

He jumped out before the propeller had stopped. He'd warned her about the dangers of getting too close to a spinning propeller and she held her breath until it slowed down. His movements seemed awkward and rushed, not at all like the smoothly competent man she'd come to know. She moved toward the ramp, eager to hear his voice as he helped the guests disembark but he ignored them and tossed their bags onto the dock.

With growing alarm she heard a raised voice from one of the men but Gray ignored him, swung up into the aircraft and was gone as abruptly as he'd arrived.

The staff member preceded the guests up the ramp, a frown on his face. It was Karl from the maintenance department. Did she imagine it, or did he refuse to look in her direction?

"Cocky young man. I think I'll have a word with Kendall about him." One of the guests spit out the words and she stepped back a few paces. The group of men passed without noticing her. They were vaguely familiar, or maybe it was just their type that was familiar. She made a mental note to have a word with their servers at dinner tonight. These customers would be demanding—and rude.

She walked back to the railing. In the few moments it took for the men to climb the ramp and go inside Gray had banked the Beaver in a right turn and was gaining altitude, heading back to Victoria. She stared after him, unable to comprehend what had just happened. There had to be a reason.

Chapter Ten

Erin turned and walked slowly into the great room. The ever-present fire crackled in the fireplace and she paused in front of it, staring into the flames. She *hadn't* been mistaken about the growing affection between herself and Gray. It was evident in the way he'd touched her, the way he'd looked into her eyes. That had been real, hadn't it? Could things have changed in only a few intervening days? She rubbed her arms, suddenly chilled by the familiar self-doubt.

Resting her head against the mantel she continued to stare into the fire. She would not allow herself to give in to those old insecurities. Besides, she'd been feeling more positive about herself every day that passed. Yes, she was disappointed not to see Gray but there must be a good reason for what had just happened. She lifted up her chin and headed for the kitchen, reminding herself that he was not like other men.

Gray was halfway to Victoria before his anger abated. He realized with a start that he'd been flying automatically, with little regard for anything other than getting away from The Lodge. Angry with himself for his inattentiveness he took note of his surroundings and changed his heading.

Since overhearing the men's conversation he'd been completely focused on his own shock, his own pain. He'd believed in his father's infidelity for so long it was hard to back up and see things from a different perspective.

How must his father have felt all these years? Gray was ashamed to realize that he'd never once considered his father's feelings. After all, in his young mind his father had hurt his mother. It had been as simple as that. Odd, he thought wryly, how when you're young everything is black and white. Clearing his mind of troubling thoughts, he checked his instruments and started the descent into Deep Cove. It was time to learn the truth.

"This is a private dock, sir." A middle-aged Asian man met him as he taxied up to the dock.

"That's all right, Jimmy." Gray looked up. His father was part way down the steep hillside. "This is my son, Gray."

David Kendall walked onto the dock, his steps unhurried. "Thank you, Jimmy." He turned to Gray. "Will you be staying for lunch?"

Gray's stomach was churning and he wasn't sure if he could eat, but he'd come this far. "That would be nice, thanks."

Hope surfaced in David Kendall's eyes and he turned to Jimmy. "Would you ask Sunny to prepare lunch for two? Thank you."

"It's good to see you, son." David Kendall held out a hand and Gray took it.

David secured the aft line to a cleat on the deck. "She's a nice one, Gray." He ran his hand along the wing. Nice paint job."

"Thank you, sir. I just added her."

"Let me guess. She'll be the workhorse, but you still prefer the Mallard."

Gray grinned. "You know it."

"Can't say I blame you."

He gestured to the steep stairs and Gray noticed that the hillside was terraced and planted with an attractive mixture of small shrubs and flowering perennials. "Nice place," he said, following his father up the hillside.

"I like it, but I can't claim credit for the gardens. Jimmy does that." He stopped at the top terrace and Gray noticed that he wasn't even breathing hard. "Jimmy and Sunny live in a cottage on the property. Sunny takes care of the house and Jimmy does everything else."

David led him onto a patio overlooking the dark green waters of Deep Cove. "Care for something cold before lunch?"

"Do you have any iced tea?" Gray gestured to the dock below. "I'm driving." He flushed, suddenly self-conscious. "I don't know why I said that. I never drink."

David shot him a quick glance then nodded. "I'll get us those drinks and check on lunch. Make yourself comfortable." He walked into the house.

Gray stared at his father's retreating back. Had he ever really known this man? Evidently not. He sat down in a comfortable chair then bounced up, restless and unsure of himself. His decision to come here had been instinctive, but was he ready for the truth? He honestly didn't know the answer.

"Here you are." His father handed him a glass of iced tea and gestured to the table. "Sunny will bring out our lunch in a few minutes."

A hummingbird appeared out of nowhere and hovered beside the table, examining the flowered centerpiece. Then it darted away to the feeder at the edge of the patio.

"Cheeky little things." David followed the tiny bird with his eyes. "But you have to admire them." He took a sip of iced tea then set down his glass. "So tell me, how is Ben's insurance claim proceeding?"

Gray was relieved to be on solid ground. "It's going well. I've been interviewed by the adjusters several times and they've also talked to Uncle Bill." He paused. "But of course you probably know that already." His father nodded. "I talked to Ben yesterday, and he says he should have the go-ahead to start shopping for a new boat within a week."

"Excellent. I spoke to Connor, and he says that Ben has arranged for someone else to deliver fuel in the meantime. We'll look forward to having him back, though." He looked up. "Ah, here's our lunch."

A striking young Asian woman appeared bearing a tray, which she set on the sideboard. With quick, efficient movements she re-arranged the table, making room for a basket of butterflake rolls and an assortment of pickles and salad dressings. Then she placed an exquisitely arranged plate of shrimp salad before Gray and his mouth watered. Perhaps he'd be able to eat after all.

"Sunny, I'd like you to meet my son, Gray."

The young woman inclined her head slightly. "Delighted to meet you," she murmured. "I hope you enjoy your lunch."

"Thank you, Sunny."

The young woman slipped from the room and his father gestured to the plate in front of him. "You used to like shrimp salad. I hope that's still the case."

The men ate in silence and Gray wondered if he'd made a mistake in coming here. His father must be wondering about his sudden arrival, but Gray hadn't glimpsed a moment's curiosity in his face. He broke the roll and bit into it, gathering his courage. Delaying the moment, he took several more forkfuls of shrimp, then put the utensil down deliberately and touched the napkin to his lips.

His father seemed to sense that the moment had come and looked up expectantly.

"Dad." His heart flooded with joy at the word and it was a moment before he could continue. "Do you know someone named Blaine Matthews?"

"Blaine?" His father frowned. "I haven't seen him for years, but yes, I know him." He seemed to steel himself.

"Your mother and I belonged to the same golf club as he and his wife, but we weren't particularly friendly. Why?"

"Because I flew him and a couple of his friends up to The Lodge this morning."

His father looked at him evenly.

Gray took a deep breath and jumped in. "They were talking among themselves and they said some nasty things about Mother." He continued before he lost his nerve. "They said she was fooling around with the golf pro."

His father's eyes flashed and Gray could see his mind working. "They didn't know who you were, obviously."

"No sir."

"Even so, that sort of talk is despicable." His nostrils flared and Gray could see that he was working hard to control his anger. "But then Matthews was never known for his good manners." He tossed down his napkin. "I'm sorry you had to hear that, son." He looked up, eyes full of pain. "And you came right here."

Gray nodded.

"Good." His father seemed far away. "That's good."

Gray waited while his father collected his thoughts. For a moment he seemed weighted down by past sorrow. Then he sat up straighter and took a deep breath.

"I haven't allowed myself to think about those days for a long time." He winced as though in pain. "Except once in a while, when I'd see you." He tried to smile.

Gray couldn't stand it any longer. "But why, Dad? All those years! Why did you let me think it was you?"

His father looked at him sadly. "Was that so wrong, son? Was it wrong to let a young boy believe in his mother?" He shook his head. "You loved your mother, and by the time I realized that you blamed me, you'd already made up your mind." The anguish in his eyes was difficult to watch. "And as time went by I almost began to believe it myself. If I hadn't been so wrapped up in my career, if I'd paid more attention to her, she might not have started drinking." He looked across to the wooded hills on the other side of the water and his voice took on a distant quality. "I always believed that I shared in the blame for her drinking. That's why I tried several times to get her into treatment. But it never worked." He pulled himself back to the present. "If I'd known that things would work out as they did, I might have acted differently. But then, what's the expression? Hindsight is always twenty-twenty? I'm just sorry I put you through all that."

"But I loved you too, Dad." Gray's throat was clogged with emotion.

His father smiled. "I knew that son. And I kept reminding myself of that fact every time you refused to look at me or to talk to me. I always believed we'd come to this point some day."

Gray slumped back in his chair. "I feel as though my whole life has been turned upside down. My head is spinning."

"Promise me one thing, son."

"What?" Gray wasn't sure he was in any state to make a promise.

"Don't think badly of your mother. Yes, she broke our marriage vows, but she never told you that I was the one who was cheating." His eyes narrowed. "Did she?"

"No." Gray shook his head, amazed that he'd never recognized that fact. "She didn't."

"I didn't think so. And by the time either of us realized what you were thinking, it was too late." He raised an eyebrow. "You were a pretty determined young fellow."

Gray thought back to those terrible days. "And angry. I doubt if I would have listened."

His father nodded. "So don't blame your mother. Okay?"

Gray nodded. It would be hard, but he'd try to do as his father asked.

"And now, I have a suggestion. If you'd like to get away, I have some business associates arriving this afternoon from Toronto. They're fanatic fishermen and when I talked to them this morning they mentioned that they'd like to go up to the Cariboo and fish one of the less accessible lakes. I told them it was late notice but that I'd check around. What do you think? Would you like to fly them up?"

Gray jumped at the chance. "A friend of mine owns the perfect spot. There's even a cabin and a boat. When do they want to leave?"

"First thing in the morning. They can only spare a couple of days. Do you think you could swing it?"

"It would be perfect." He did a quick mental check of his upcoming charters. "Besides, it's the incentive I needed to hook up with another pilot and I know just the fellow to take over while I'm gone. I'll get going now and line things up."

"Sounds good." His father stood up. "I'll let you get

on with it then." He took a step forward. "Gray, thanks for coming."

Gray stepped into his father's arms, gave him a fierce hug and then turned away to swipe at the moisture in his eyes. He headed down the steps and turned at the first terrace to look back. His father was still watching him. "Thanks, Dad." The words filled what had been an empty spot in his soul. He grinned and then ran the rest of the way down to the dock.

"Chef! Have you seen the paper?" The sous-chef waved a folded newspaper in the air.

Erin looked up. "Afraid not, Paul. I haven't looked at a newspaper since I got here." She returned her attention to the torte on a rotating stand. The pastry chef had been called away on a family emergency and she'd been only too happy to fill in, hoping that the extra duties would keep her from thinking about Gray. It hadn't worked. "What have I been missing?"

"Oh nothing much." The sous-chef snapped the paper and adjusted his glasses, looking around to make sure he had the attention of everyone in the kitchen. "The headline reads: *Local Chef Saves The Day.*" He lowered the paper. "Now who would that be, I wonder?"

Erin's head snapped up. "Please tell me that story isn't about me."

The sous-chef shrugged. "Sorry."

"I don't believe it!" Erin waved a spatula in the air and mocha icing flew against the wall. "How could anyone write a story like that without at least interviewing the people involved? Which newspaper is that, anyway?"

The sous-chef tapped the masthead. "*The West Coast Gazette.* It's an offshoot of one of the big dailies. Shall I go on?"

Erin groaned knowing it wouldn't do any good to object.

In today's modern world, where 'behaving badly' has become an art form, there are still angels among us. Genuine flesh and blood angels with the compassion and strength of character to turn what might have been an ordeal into a pleasant interlude for the writer.

"Shall I continue?"

Erin piped icing onto the torte. "Does it say who wrote that nonsense?"

"Let's see. Oh yes, there's a photo and everything. Bill Corbett. Friend of yours?"

Erin couldn't believe her ears. "Bill? I don't believe it." She paused. "There must be some mistake." She finished icing the torte and peered over the sous-chef's shoulder. "But how? He was on the boat with us when we had the accident. Is this newspaper so desperate for stories that they let anybody write for them?"

"But *chérie,* he's not just anybody. We all know Bill Corbett. He's a friend of David Kendall and he's a frequent visitor to The Lodge." Paul was enjoying the moment.

"Yes but what does that have to do with the newspaper?" Erin was beginning to feel desperate.

"Simple. He's the publisher. He owns it."

"He owns it? Bill?" Erin thought for a moment. "But when we were on the boat he said he was in communications."

"And so he is. He's been writing a column in the *Gazette* for years. What better way to communicate, *non?*" Paul's French background was coming through in his language.

Erin couldn't help but smile. Both she and Angela had assumed that Bill meant telecommunications, and he hadn't corrected them. "Wait 'till I get ahold of him," she murmured, but the heat had gone out of her words.

"Oh la! You haven't heard the best part yet. He goes on to say how you rowed the boat to shore, built a fire pit, put up a shelter and after all that, you cooked mussels for dinner. A regular Robertson Crusoe!"

"Robinson Crusoe." Erin corrected him automatically. "But I wasn't the only one. Angela helped. Gray, too." She looked around at her co-workers. "We all worked together. We really did."

"He talks about all that, but you were definitely the star of the show. No doubt about it."

Paul finally relinquished the newspaper and Erin sat on the steps leading up to her office, reading the article. Bill's words were simple and straightforward, effortlessly capturing the essence of those days. She could almost smell the kelp as it sizzled in the fire and taste the tea in those ridiculous little collapsible cups.

"It doesn't matter," she said aloud, not caring if anyone was listening. She'd just finished reading the article for the second time. "As long as the others aren't offended, that is." She folded the newspaper and tossed it in the recycling bin. "I don't know what I was so worried about. A few people will read it, then it will blow over."

Gray stepped out of the cabin just as the call of a loon echoed down the lake. His father had been right. This short trip had been exactly what he needed to get his head back on straight. His father's business associates were still asleep and he sat down on the front steps of the cabin, watching the underside of the clouds change from pale pink to gold as the sun rose. Several other cabins dotted the shoreline of the remote lake, but none were occupied at the moment.

The loon's mate answered, its warbling call floating through the still air. Yesterday, after they'd arrived, his father's two business associates had hauled the boat out from under the cabin and launched it, preferring to use the oars rather than the trolling motor. For the first hour they'd seen very little action but as the afternoon wore on and the temperature cooled down the fish started biting. As with most anglers in the area they had practiced catch and release, except for three trout, which were earmarked for dinner. Along with corn and potatoes cooked in the fire, the pan-fried trout made for a satisfying meal.

He wasn't one for introspection, but he couldn't help but wish that he hadn't wasted all those years hating his father. The past couldn't be reversed, but he vowed to make up for it. From now on, his father would be part of his life. And he hoped that that life would also include Erin.

He sauntered down to the firepit at the edge of the water. Warmth still radiated from the embers, and he threw on a few more pieces of wood, prodding it with a stick. Last night he'd sat out here long after the others had retired, needing the luxury of silence to think about his life—his past and his future. From now on, sitting beside a fire would always remind him of Erin. He'd been selfish to take off the way he did, leaving her without a clue as to why he'd left The Lodge so abruptly. He owed her an apology but it was something that had to be done in person. There was too much to explain. He only hoped that she would forgive him when he got back.

"Telephone for you, Chef." Yvonne wiggled the handset.

Erin pointed to her office and Yvonne nodded. Heart racing, she sat down and composed herself before picking up the handset. It had been two days since Gray left and every time the phone rang she'd answered it breathlessly, hoping to hear his voice.

"Hello?" She heard some noise in the background. "Erin Delaney here."

"One moment please Miss Delaney. Jonathan Forbes would like to talk to you."

Erin frowned at the telephone. She disliked people who couldn't make their own telephone calls. The name Jonathan Forbes was vaguely familiar, but she couldn't place it.

"Hello, Miss Delaney?"

"Yes."

"Jonathan Forbes here."

She scribbled his name on a piece of paper, waiting for him to continue but he remained silent, as though he was waiting for her to react. "Can I help you, Mr. Forbes?"

"I've been reading about you in the *Gazette*, Miss Delaney." He paused. "May I call you Erin?" He didn't wait for a response. "You see, Erin, we think what you did is remarkable, and we'd like to do a piece on you for our weekend *Newsmagazine*. Four people shipwrecked on a remote beach." His voice rose dramatically. "Living on nothing but their wits. Forced to boil water in an old can and survive on mussels wrapped in seaweed." She could hear the crackle of newspaper in the background. "It's a reality show played out on the coast of British Columbia."

"No thanks . . ." she looked down at her note . . . "Jonathan. One article on our adventure is plenty, thank you very much."

He laughed. It sounded forced and Erin envisioned him in front of the mirror, trying it out. "No, no. I'm talking about CHIC's *Sunday Newsmagazine* program. It's one of the most watched programs on our station."

"In that case, I'm *really* not interested. But thank you."

He carried on as thought he hadn't heard. "We thought we'd get the four of you together for an interview and I've already spoken with Bill Corbett. He warned me you'd be hard to convince."

Erin smiled to herself. "Well he was right." She tried to remain pleasant, remembering her position at The Lodge. "Did Bill say he'd be willing to do it?"

The reporter hesitated. "He promised to give me an answer one way or the other at the end of the day but I think he's leaning our way. So far only Mrs. Siebring has given me a positive answer."

"Mrs. Siebring?"

"Yes, Angela Siebring. She seems eager to sing your praises."

"What about Gray?" Erin caught herself. "Graydon Kendall."

"Well, it seems that Mr. Kendall is on a charter at the moment. He's expected back some time today and I have a call in to him the moment he lands."

Erin absorbed this information but it didn't change how she felt about appearing on television. "I'm sorry to disappoint you, Mr. Forbes, but as I said I'm not interested."

"You could view it as a public service." He was starting to sound desperate. "We're going to do a few minutes on survival. You know, tips on how people can survive in similar circumstances."

"Mr. Forbes." Erin couldn't keep the impatience out of her voice. "We were only on that beach for two nights. We were hardly in any danger."

"Yes but you were the lucky ones. What of others who might not be so fortunate?"

"I suppose you have a point."

"Thank you. By the way I spoke with your sister this afternoon and she seems to think you're a real hero."

"Crystal? You spoke to my sister Crystal?" Erin felt her body go rigid. "Why did you do that?"

"Background, Miss Delaney. It's how we build a piece."

Erin looked around desperately. She didn't want to

get into a discussion about Crystal. "I see. Well thank you for calling, Mr. Forbes."

"I can't talk you into it?"

"I'm afraid not." She hoped she sounded firm. "Good-bye, Mr. Forbes."

"Good-bye Erin. If you change your mind, call me. Any time."

Erin slowly replaced the handset, thoughts racing around inside her head. Was she being dog-in-the-mangerish? Not wanting to appear on television, but not wanting Crystal to represent her, either? She felt a headache coming on and rummaged through her drawer for some aspirin. She took the pill, swallowing it with a long drink from her water bottle. Why didn't she want to appear on television? She knew the answer, but didn't want to admit it. Didn't want to admit that she was still insecure about her appearance. She lowered her head into her hands. Would she ever be able to see past the old Erin and recognize the new person who had emerged? She wasn't sure.

Gray flew the two men back to his father's home. Quite the opposite from his last trip, the men had been easy going and appreciative. His father came down to the dock and invited him in but he declined. "I'll call you later though and thanks for the idea. It did the trick."

His father nodded and clapped him in the shoulder. "Good, I'm glad."

Gray took off and headed out over the ocean, flying along the coastline en route to the inner harbour and his base. There was one last thing he wanted to do. Passing the exclusive area known as Uplands, he found what he'd been looking for—the waterfront estate where he'd grown up. Looking down on the familiar buildings, his life seemed to play out in fast forward—the happiness of his youth followed by the pain and anger of his teenage years. And then he was past. This fly-by marked a pivotal point in his life. From now on, he would hold on to the happy times and leave the hurt behind. It felt good. He wished he could keep on flying and share it all with Erin.

He set the aircraft down in the busy inner harbour and taxied to his dock. Colin came out of the tiny office and helped him tie down behind the Beaver.

"Everything okay here?" He greeted the new pilot. "How were the flights?"

"Great. "Wow, that lodge is something. Your father's one smart guy."

Gray nodded. The floating fishing lodge had been an innovative concept, and for the first time he acknowledged his father's genius.

"You're popular today. The phone's been ringing off the hook."

Gray frowned. "Really? What's up?"

"I don't know. Ben wants you to call, and some guy from a television station called, and somebody called Bill Corbett said you should call him before you talk to anybody." He paused to catch his breath. "And there have been a couple of calls regarding charters. I looked in your book and didn't see anything else so I took the charters and told them we'd reconfirm later today."

"Good, good." Gray strode toward the office. "Did Bill say what's so all-fired important?"

"No, and I didn't ask. He sounds like he knows you, though."

"Yeah. He's my godfather."

"Now I remember where I heard his name. He was with you when the boat went up, wasn't he?"

Gray looked puzzled. "How did you know that?"

"He wrote an article in the *Gazette*. Tells how you all survived. That chef sure sounds like quite the woman."

"Forget it, she's taken," Gray growled.

"Huh. It didn't sound like it." Colin opened his mouth to continue, then saw the expression on Gray's face. "Oh, I see. Fair enough."

"Maybe I should qualify that. She's taken but she doesn't know it yet."

"Well, my man, maybe you should tell her. Everybody's talking about it."

Gray shook his head. "Let's check those charters you took, then you can call and reconfirm while I call Uncle Bill."

Chapter Eleven

"Gray, my boy, thanks for calling." Bill sounded like his old self. "You haven't talked to CHIC yet, have you?"

"No, I just got back. How are you feeling? You sound great."

"Never better, but it seems I've stirred up a bit of a hornet's nest with that article I wrote."

"So I hear, but what's so urgent?"

"CHIC wants to do a story on the four of us for that program they air on Sundays. I think it's called *Sunday Newsmagazine*. I had no idea the article would stir up so much interest."

"What did you say?"

"Just the truth. That we all pulled together, but that it was Erin who kept us going."

Gray grunted. "Sounds about right."

"The thing is, Angela has said she'll be on the program, but I wanted to talk to you before I agreed. I don't think it would do any harm, but the producer called me back about half an hour ago and said that Erin doesn't want anything to do with it."

"Why not?"

"She didn't say. They really want her, of course, and this guy Jonathan Forbes doesn't give up easily. Know what he's done? He called Erin's sister."

"Uh oh."

"Exactly. And he says if Erin won't come they'll probably interview her sister instead."

"The sister's agreed?" Gray was beginning to get a headache.

"I don't know, but he suggested as much."

"Erin isn't going to like this."

"That's just it. And the guy's a bit of a weasel. He'll probably tell her they're thinking of using her sister." Bill's tone made it clear he was unhappy with the way things were proceeding.

"Why is Erin being so stubborn?"

"Well, son, I've been thinking about that. We both know that she's a very capable woman, but when it comes to her personal life, she lacks self-confidence. The way I read it, she focused all her attention on her sister and neglected herself. She's an attractive woman, but she doesn't know it."

Gray exhaled slowly, thinking back to the afternoon he'd spent with Erin at the hot pools. "I think you're right. She said her sister's become self-centered, and believe it or not, she blames herself. I'd hate to see Crystal steal her thunder on this, but if she doesn't want to come, what can we do?"

"What if you called her? Do you think she'd agree then?"

Gray was silent for several moments. "I don't think so. I had a date with her earlier in the week. We were supposed to have coffee together, but that was the day I flew those three men up, and I was so angry I couldn't talk. I have to explain it to her, but it's not something that can be done over the phone."

"Your dad told me. I'm sorry you had to hear about it like that, but at least you've resolved your differences. It means a lot to him."

"Me too."

"Now, back to the problem at hand. We could agree to go on the program. If we do that, we can make sure that Erin gets the credit she deserves."

"I'm not crazy about being on television, but you're right. I'd go up to see her if I could, but the charters have been pouring in. Both planes are busy tomorrow. Colin's taking some government type to the Fraser River where they're touring a couple of mills, and I'm off to Seattle."

"Sounds like business is good. So are we agreed then? We'll do their interview?"

"When is it?" Gray checked his calendar.

"The day after tomorrow."

"Okay. I'll call them now."

"Mr. Kendall? Thank you for calling back."

The television producer made his pitch and Gray listened patiently. "All right, I'll do it."

There was a moment's hesitation. "Wonderful. Now

I'm hoping we can impose on you for one more thing. We'd like to do a very short promotional piece. A teaser, we call it. Would you be available for just a few minutes this afternoon?"

Gray glanced at his watch. "Afraid not, Larry. I'm busy here getting ready for a flight tomorrow."

"In that case, we could come to you." The producer wasn't going to give up. "It will only take a minute or two, and it would be a nice bit of publicity for your business. We could shoot on the dock, with your planes in the background."

Gray looked out the window at his fleet of two. "Okay. I'll be here for another hour."

"Great. See you in half an hour."

"Erin, look at this." The kitchen had slowed down after the dinner rush, and someone had turned on the small television mounted on the wall. "It's Gray. He's on television." Paul turned up the volume. "And who is that?"

Every eye in the kitchen was focused on the television screen. Erin recognized the voice of the reporter who had called her, but her attention was riveted on the two people he was interviewing.

It couldn't be! She took a step closer to the television, stifling a gasp. Gray and Crystal stood side by side on a dock, Gray's float planes in the background. Erin shivered, suddenly cold.

On the screen a passing yacht sent waves lapping under the dock and Crystal clutched at Gray's arm. Erin watched his face intently as he steadied her, but could not detect a reaction. Her heart thundered in her ears and she missed the first few words of Crystal's response.

". . . in the fashion industry, but what I'd really like is to become a model."

"And your sister?" Jonathan Forbes ran a hand over his hair as the wind caught it.

"Erin? Oh no, she's never been interested in modeling." Crystal turned to Gray. "But she is a good cook, wouldn't you say, Gray?"

"Erin is a fully qualified chef de cuisine, but it was more than her cooking skills that helped us over a rough time." He looked directly into the camera. "She's an amazing woman."

Crystal looked up at him with adoring eyes. "Yes, amazing."

The camera switched to Jonathan Forbes. "And we hope you'll join us at five o'clock on Sunday afternoon for this week's edition of *Sunday Newsmagazine.*"

"You're going to be on television?" Paul looked at her, wide-eyed.

Erin shook her head, too stunned to reply. She walked to her office on wooden legs and slumped into her chair.

Her telephone buzzed and she picked it up listlessly.

"Erin, tell me you saw that piece they just did on television!" Angela's excited voice was a welcome distraction. "You've got to change your mind and agree to appear."

"Why?" Erin couldn't think straight. She could still see the way Crystal had looked at Gray. "Why did you agree to do it?"

"Because." Angela drew the word out. "They made it sound like you'd already agreed and I wanted to be there to make sure everyone knows how you saved us all."

"Oh come on, Angela. It wasn't like that and you know it." Erin pulled off her beanie and tossed it on the desk. "This whole thing has become a circus."

"I agree, it has, a bit. So why don't you surprise everybody and come down for the taping? You could set the record straight." Angela paused. "Otherwise your sister will speak for you."

Erin stood up. "I wouldn't mind that so much. She just wants a bit of attention." She tried to laugh. "What do they call it? Face time?"

"Seems to me she had that tonight. Besides, did you see the way she was mooning at Gray? Come on, Erin. Whatever happened to the strong woman I met on the boat?"

Erin caught a glimpse of her reflection in the window and laughed. "She's fading away."

"Fading away? What's that supposed to mean?"

"It's all your fault, you know. I've started working out." Erin turned sideways, admiring her new figure. "I'm going to have to get my chef's pants taken in and I've actually got cheekbones."

"That settles it!"

"What do you mean?"

"You're coming. That's all there is to it." Erin could almost hear her thinking. "The taping's scheduled for the day after tomorrow. You'll fly down tomorrow, I'll pick you up and we'll go shopping."

"Angela, I really don't want to see Crystal right now."

"You'll stay here, with me. It'll be fun. Come on, Erin. Say you'll do it."

The television set flickered on the wall. "All right,

I'm due for a few days off. There's a lodge charter leaving in the morning. I'll call you back in half an hour and tell you what time."

Angela greeted her with open arms. "Can you believe this weather? Nothing but sun for the past week. I love it." She gave Erin a crushing hug then held her at arm's length. "Girlfriend, you look wonderful."

"You think so?"

"Absolutely. Let's go shopping!"

"That's the one." Angela stepped back and admired Erin. "Your hair looks fabulous against that color of green. It's inspired and it'll look great on television." She adjusted the collar of the suit. "You'll wear it without a blouse, and we'll find an elegant necklace."

"Me? Elegant? You've gotta be kidding!" Erin laughed.

Angela waved a hand dismissively. "I've never been more serious. Now, let's look for a little black dress."

"A little black dress? Whatever for?"

"It's something you should have. Besides, Daniel's taking us out to morrow after the taping. I have no idea why they have to do it so late in the day, but it works out well. Danny's going to escort us to McMorrans."

"McMorrans? But they have dancing there and everything. I'll stand out like a bump on a log." Erin was starting to panic.

"We don't have to dance. Besides, I thought you'd like to study their menu. They do a terrific crab cake."

"I give up." Erin trudged along behind Angela like a

dutiful child and they selected a simple black dress with a scooped neck and a slightly flared skirt. She stared at her reflection in the mirror of the dressing room, hardly recognizing herself.

"Now. Shoes, jewelry, and then we're finished." Angela raised an eyebrow. "You do wear high heels, don't you?"

Erin caught a glimpse of herself in a mirror and tossed her hair. "The old Erin didn't, but this one does."

Angela paced back and forth in front of the window, watching for Daniel's car. "He's not usually late like this," she moaned, checking her watch again. "I hope he's all right."

"He's only ten minutes late." Erin stood up to calm her friend. "Wait a minute. I see lights coming up the driveway now."

"I'm really sorry." Daniel greeted Angela with a kiss. "But I was in the middle of delicate negotiations."

Angela hustled them all into the car. "We're not too late. Let's hope they wait."

Daniel concentrated on driving and fifteen minutes later he steered the car into the underground parking lot.

The receptionist in the lobby checked a screen and frowned. "Studio three," she said hesitantly. "But I think they've already started taping."

A red light glowed over the door marked STUDIO THREE and Angela peeked in the narrow window. "There's Bill," she said excitedly. "And Gray."

She moved aside and Erin looked in. "And Crystal." She couldn't tell if the interview had commenced but

Crystal was laughing, her hand on Gray's arm. It was the second time she'd seen Crystal touch him. It had started the same way with Dominic. Flashing eyes, laughter, the gentle pressure of a hand. She turned away. "This was a mistake," she said, her voice tense. "I don't think I can do it."

"Nonsense." Angela pushed the door open and grabbed her friend by the arm. She was surprisingly strong.

"Sorry we're late." Angela walked past the cameras and smiled at Jonathan Forbes, extending her hand. "Angela Siebring." She turned around. "And Erin Delaney."

"Erin!" Bill stepped down from the set, a broad smile on his face. "What a surprise. Are we glad to see you!"

"Erin?" Crystal stared at her sister. "Is that you?"

"Well!" Jonathan Forbes rose from his position between Bill and Gray. "This is marvelous." He prowled around Erin in a semicircle. "What made you change your mind?"

Erin smiled at Angela. "My friend," she said simply. She turned to her sister. "Hello, Crystal."

Crystal was still staring. "Erin, you look wonderful." She sat beside Gray, her blond hair luminous in the glare of the television lights.

"Thank you." Erin glanced at Gray. He was watching the interaction intently and rose slowly. "I'm glad to see you," he said quietly.

Erin searched his eyes but there was no message there. Had it happened again? Had Crystal managed to ensnare him? She turned away, blinking back tears of frustration. The producer bustled forward. "I'm sorry to rush you, but we only have this studio for another forty-five minutes. He looked closely at Angela and Erin. "Your makeup is perfect."

"Yes, I did it." Angela acknowledged the compliment.

A sound technician clipped mikes to their clothes and the producer guided them toward the set. "Then perhaps we should get seated and start again." Catching Jonathan's eye he led Crystal aside while the interviewer placed Erin on his right, and the others took their seats.

"Now," said Jonathan with obvious relish, "let's hear about this adventure of yours."

"That wasn't so bad." Angela turned to Bill after the taping. "But promise me one thing, my friend. Next time we get shipwrecked, please don't write a story about it."

"I promise." He smiled fondly at the slender blond then turned to Erin. "We weren't too hard on you, were we?" He indicated Gray with a nod of his head. "We wanted to make sure that your side of the story was heard."

"You were great." Crystal appeared at Erin's side, eyes sparkling with excitement. "Did you really clean a fish?"

Erin laughed. "Crystal, I'm a chef, remember?"

Daniel appeared beside Erin. "Our reservation is in forty minutes and you girls still have to change. Sorry to break up the party, but we'd better get going."

"My goodness, yes." Angela gave Bill a peck on the cheek. "You take care of yourself, my friend." She turned to Crystal. "Do you have a ride home?"

"Oh, Gray is taking me." She looked across the studio to where Gray was in conversation with Jonathan Forbes. "No problem."

Angela hustled Erin out of the studio. "Come on then, we just have time to get home, change, and make it to the restaurant."

Erin changed her clothes, scarcely aware of what she was doing. Standing in front of the mirror she smoothed her new dress over her newly slender figure. She wasn't a fat girl any more, but it didn't seem to make any difference. She put on her earrings automatically, hardly noticing the way the crystal chandeliers hung alongside her neck, peeking out through the riotous mass of hair. What had Gray seen when he looked at her? She grabbed her bag and left the bedroom, suddenly afraid of the answer.

"Angela, you haven't changed your clothes." Her friend waited by the front door. "I thought you were going to wear a dress."

"Changed my mind," she answered blithely. "Come on, we'll be late."

Erin stared dully out the window as the car wove through traffic. She'd tried one last time to catch Gray's eye on their way out of the studio but he hadn't responded. Her heart lay in her chest like a heavy rock.

The sun was hovering just above the horizon when Daniel pulled up in front of the restaurant.

"Here we are." Angela jumped out before the doorman could get to the car. "Erin and I will go in while you park the car."

The maitre d' greeted Angela warmly. "Mrs. Siebring. Good to see you again." He gestured for them to follow him. "Your table is ready. This way please."

"Go on," said Angela. "I'm right behind you."

Erin forced herself to walk through the crowded room, aware of the admiring looks cast in her direction. Through the windows, the surf creamed gently against the beach, golden in the glow of the setting sun. What was she doing here? It was a setting for lovers.

"Your table, madam." The maitre d' stood aside and Erin gasped. Gray rose from the table, a devilish smile on his face.

Erin turned around. Angela had disappeared.

"Gray?" A delightful warmth spread through her body. "What . . . what are you doing here?"

"I came to have dinner with my girl." He pulled out her chair and she sat down. His hand brushed her shoulder. "You are my girl, aren't you?"

She felt a blush creep up her neck but she didn't care. She didn't care if the whole world knew how she felt about this man. "Are you asking me to be your girl?"

He reached across the table and took her hand. "Yes," he said, his voice husky.

"But . . ." She fluttered a hand in front of her face then dropped her eyes. "I thought maybe Crystal . . ."

"Erin, look at me." He squeezed her fingers gently. "Your sister is a natural flirt. She can't help it, but I'm a one-woman man." He paused. "And you're that woman."

"I am?" She raised her head to find him looking at her with an expression that left her breathless. "Oh."

He looked up at a hovering waiter. "Would you please

bring us a couple of mineral waters with a twist and then leave us alone for a while? We have a lot of talking to do."

He turned back to her. "I had dinner with your sister last night."

Erin's head shot up.

He saw the question in her eyes. "Fish and chips at Barb's. Then I dropped her off. The point is, I think she's changed." He shrugged. "Well, maybe not completely. She's still wrapped up in herself, but she's beginning to understand how much you did for her, and how much she relied on you. I get the impression she's grown up a lot since you've been away."

"Oh Gray, I hope so. That's one of the reasons I left."

"And the others?"

She looked out the window and thought back to the person she had been. "Believe it or not, I wanted a bit of an adventure. I wanted to do something that was only for myself."

"Well you certainly succeeded."

"I did, didn't I?" She smiled at him, suddenly confident. "You know, if that offer is still open, the answer is yes. I'd like to be your girl, but promise me one thing, okay? Please don't ever stand me up again." She leaned forward, suddenly serious. "What happened Gray? Why did you leave in such a hurry?"

He told her the story and a tear rolled down her cheek. "All those years," she said, reaching for his hand. "But they're in the past now."

He nodded. "So you see, you were right to have faith in my father. Turns out he's a good man after all."

"And so are you Gray. She allowed her eyes to roam over his face, memorizing every detail. "A very good man."

The music started and he stood up, his hand extended. "May I have this dance?"

She looked up at him, startled. "I thought you didn't dance."

"I didn't say that." He pulled her into his arms. "I said I'm not all that good ány more."

They moved across the dance floor as if they'd been dancing together forever. His arms tightened, and he lowered his head until his mouth was by her ear. "How am I doing?" he asked softly.

"Fine," she replied. "Just fine." A small sigh escaped her lips. "It's as though we've been dancing together forever. And right now no one else exists."

He pulled her hand to his lips. The touch was electric. "They don't."

She looked into his eyes, seeing endless horizons. "I think I like that."